DARK LEGACY
THE LEGACY SERIES

JEN TALTY

JUPITER PRESS

"Deadly Secrets is the best of romance and suspense in one hot read!" *NYT Bestselling Author Jennifer Probst*

"A charming setting and a steamy couple heat up the pages in a suspenseful story I couldn't put down!" *NY Times and USA today Bestselling Author Donna Grant*

"Jen Talty's books will grab your attention and pull you into a world of relatable characters, strong personalities, humor, and believable storylines. You'll laugh, you'll cry, and you'll rush to get the next book she releases!" Natalie Ann USA Today Bestselling Author

"I positively loved *In Two Weeks*, and highly recommend it. The writing is wonderful, the story is fantastic, and the characters will keep you coming back for more. I can't wait to get my hands on future installments of the NYS Troopers series." *Long and Short Reviews*

"*In Two Weeks* hooks the reader from page one. This is a fast paced story where the development of the romance grabs you emotionally and the suspense keeps you sitting on the edge of your chair. Great characters, great writing, and a believable plot that can be a warning to all of us." *Desiree Holt, USA Today Bestseller*

"*Dark Water* delivers an engaging portrait of wounded hearts as the memorable characters take you on a healing journey of love. A mysterious death brings danger and intrigue into the drama, while sultry passions brew into a believable plot that melts the reader's heart. Jen Talty pens an entertaining romance that grips the heart as the colorful and dangerous story unfolds into a chilling ending." *Night Owl Reviews*

"This is not the typical love story, nor is it the typical mystery. The characters are well rounded and interesting." *You Gotta Read Reviews*

"*Murder in Paradise Bay* is a fast-paced romantic thriller with plenty of twists and turns to keep you guessing until the end. You won't want to miss this one..." *USA Today bestselling author Janice Maynard*

DARK LEGACY

The Legacy Series book 1

USA Today Bestselling Author
JEN TALTY

PROLOGUE

Life without hope was not a life worthy of breath.

Or so Shannon Brendel's mother had said. Shannon had never forgotten it, but some days, she wished she'd never heard it.

Today was one of those days.

She sat by the bedroom window of her father's summer home in Lake George, New York. The tall mast of her dad's pride and joy rattled in the slight breeze. The new Tartan had been the bane of her existence in more ways than one. She'd lost her childhood on that boat.

And her father had allowed it to happen. Hell, he'd orchestrated the entire thing.

She contemplated for the millionth time what it would be like if she slipped into the darkness and disappeared. No one would really miss her. Her family didn't understand the concept of caring for those you were supposed to love. Her friends weren't really friends—more people she hid behind. If she were to die, her passing would simply be a little blip on the radar, and then everyone's life would likely go on as if nothing had happened.

She closed her eyes, letting the darkness fill her mind. She remembered the feeling of being put under anesthesia. It was as if you simply faded to black—total unawareness.

That is exactly what she wanted.

That had been the best feeling ever, and she wanted it again, only she didn't want the waking-up part.

While she sat there in search of obscurity, she heard her mother's voice somewhere in the recesses of her mind. It haunted her like a bad song that she couldn't get out of her head.

Everything will be better tomorrow, you'll see. When you wake up, things will be different.

Lies. It was all lies. But the problem was, part of Shannon wanted to believe her mother's false truths.

Shannon blinked, allowing reality to bombared her brain like a pack of wild wolves racing through the woods, hunting their prey. She slid open the window in the bedroom her father allowed her to stay in when the *wayward student* paid him a visit—which was far too often if you asked her. Being with her father wasn't any worse than being at her mother's. Although many, if they knew the truth, would think differently.

At least her father noticed her existence. She supposed that counted for something.

The wind was still, and it was a whopping fifty-degrees outside. It wasn't really cold, but the air was crisp enough to give her chills. Stars filled the night sky, and the moon almost looked bright like the sun as it cast its glow over the sailboat taunting her—almost laughing at her from the water only a few hundred feet away.

She rubbed her stomach. The memory of the physical pain had slipped away, but the baby's piercing cry would be forever etched in her memory. Her father hadn't enforced his visitation rights in months. Now that her little problem was gone and no signs of her existence remained, her father wanted his princess back in his twisted, sick world.

"I did the right thing," she whispered.

Headlights appeared in the distance. Three cars slowly drove past. She wished she had the courage to step out into the night, stick out her thumb, and hitch a ride to a new beginning.

Everything would be different tomorrow.

She quickly closed the window. Her shoulder-length, dark-blond hair blew across her face.

It was nearly midnight, and her wicked stepmonster —though Annette wasn't really the worst person in the world—and father had long ago gone to bed. Having a teenager in the house was too much for the poor woman, and her father hadn't been too thrilled with having to entertain a few of the neighbors, so he'd gotten drunk and passed out early.

Thank God.

Shannon opened the closet. Her blanket and teddy bear were safe. So was her bottle of mother's little helpers. Maybe tonight she'd find the courage.

But what if you wake tomorrow and it's all different?

"Damn you, Mother." She locked her door. She might pay for it with a black eye, but she didn't want a visitor at three in the morning.

She climbed into the closet, closed the door, and hugged her teddy. She fiddled with the bottle of pills. She'd hold onto them all night, never taking a single one.

Wishing she could.

Tomorrow, everything would be different.

———

Shannon woke the next morning, forcing herself to believe that the day was filled with promise and hope— even though she knew, deep down, that nothing was different.

Everything was exactly as it had been yesterday.

And that stupid damn boat was still docked out in front of her window, reminding her that her life would never be hers.

She dressed in her favorite jeans and a V-neck shirt. When she went to the kitchen, her stepmonster,

Annette, sat at the table, coffee in one hand and a smoke in the other.

The only reason Shannon had given Annette the nickname was because who in their right mind would willingly marry Dwight Brendel? Sadly, poor Annette had been snowed like so many other women, and now she was stuck in the never-ending insanity with no way out.

"You don't smoke. You hate smoking," Shannon said.

"Some events in life are worth lighting a cancer stick," Annette said in her best Southern drawl. A single tear streaked down her cheek.

"I don't much like spending the day with my father's side of the family, either," Shannon said as she got a diet soda out of the fridge. "Loud group of mother-fucking perverts, but it's only one day, and you never know...we might have fun. It's certainly not worth crying over."

"Don't swear, dear. I hate it when you swear. It's not ladylike."

Shannon sat down next to the monster and realized the woman hadn't showered or put on makeup, which was more than odd. It was downright blasphemous. "You look like shit." Shannon had never seen Annette without her extra-long eyelashes, bright lipstick, and her bleached-blond hair perfectly styled. She was the kind of woman who never left the house without her face on. It took a lot of money to make a woman look that cheap.

When Annette had taken up bowling, she bought only the finest equipment. Same went for cross-country skiing. Shannon's father would get all bent out of shape about the bill and the fact that his wife would neither stay with the activities nor be any good at them. Annette would tilt her head, bat her lashes, and say in the sweetest Southern accent she could muster, "Honey bear, it doesn't matter if I'm any good. All that matters is if I look good doing it."

Shannon watched her stepmother take a long drag off her cigarette. It was weird to watch her smoke. Almost as if she'd woken up in an alternate universe.

"Have you ever noticed that your father always forgets to turn off the light at the end of the dock?" Annette pointed toward the lakefront.

Shannon forced her gaze to the forty-foot Tartan moored in front of the house, the words *Blew by You* displayed proudly on the stern. "He wants everyone to think he's so clever with the name of his boat."

"You're probably right," Annette said. "Sugar, there's a bottle of vodka above the microwave. Would you be a doll and get it for me?"

"Since when do you drink in the morning?"

Annette could knock them back with the best of them, but where her father always lived by the rule that it was five o'clock somewhere, Annette preferred the five o'clock in whatever time zone she was in and never broke it.

Never.

Shannon did as instructed. When she first met the stepmonster, she'd thought that what Annette wanted, Annette got. However, the more she got to know the woman, she realized hatt she wasn't as shallow as Shannon had first thought. "You're kind of freaking me out."

"Tragedy will do that to some people."

Shannon placed the bottle in front of Annette and then asked, "What kind of tragedy?"

"Death."

"Who died?" Shannon asked. Her heart filled with a combination of sorrow...

And excitement.

She held her breath.

"Your father."

Shannon paused. Her mouth dropped open as if to scream. Her stomach bottomed out. She breathed in deeply. Held it. Then exhaled. This couldn't be happening, could it?

"Yeah, right. That man will outlive us all. He's already proven that after having two heart attacks before he hit forty-five." She reached for the bottle of vodka, poured some into her soda, and then gulped. "Seriously, who died?"

Annette poured a hefty amount of alcohol into her coffee "Your father. He's dead. Really dead." Her body shook. She downed the coffee and then looked directly into Shannon's eyes. "I'm sorry." Annette lowered her gaze. "And not just that he's dead, but for, well...I'm just sorry."

Shannon burst out laughing. She knew it wasn't funny. And she did feel bad. Sort of. Well, she felt bad in a weird way. For Annette.

"This is not funny. None of it is funny. I loved him. Even when I found...even when I didn't want to know about it all. I still loved him."

Shannon couldn't stop laughing. "I'm sorry," she said. "This is a defense mechanism." The more she talked, the less she laughed. She figured she'd better keep talking. "When I was little, my uncle Ned backed over my... my... it doesn't matter. I laughed when I should have cried."

"This is quite different, dear," Annette said.

"I know." The laughter had stopped, but tears had not replaced it. She was sad. At least, she thought she was. She should be filled with grief, but an over-whelming sense of relief made sadness something just out of reach.

Had tomorrow finally come?

That thought chilled her to the bone. If he was dead, truly dead, what did that really mean? Her life as she knew it would be different. Not different like moving, but different in an earth-shattering way.

She had dreamt of what her life might look like if her father weren't in the picture. But now that her reality might shift, she wasn't so sure she wanted another twist and turn of the roller coaster.

"Are you sure he's dead? He was drunker than a skunk, and you know how that man sleeps like a rock when he's completely wasted."

"He's always completely wasted."

Annette had a point, but Shannon wasn't satisfied. "How do you know he's dead? I mean, really dead?"

Annette glared. "You can go look if you want. He's in bed. Ambulance should have been here by now. Damn 9-1-1 person wanted me to try to perform CPR, but he's cold and stiff, and I couldn't stand to be in that room one second longer with a dead man. God only knows how long I slept next to him that way."

That sounded pretty dead. "Shit."

The monster started bawling. Silently, no less. Her shoulders bounced up and down, tears pouring out of her eyes, but she hardly made any noise.

Shannon awkwardly patted the woman on the back. The monster hadn't ever been particularly affectionate —which was fine with Shannon—but that left her a lack of desire for closeness in her life.

Sirens blared down the street.

Her father was dead.

Gone.

Finally.

Shannon sat down and put her arms around Annette. In return, Annette squeezed her so tightly that Shannon started to cry.

Real tears.

They weren't for her father. Not really. She'd

honestly wished him dead many times. She doubted she'd miss him but knew her life had just changed fundamentally. She cried harder.

Once Annette let the police, paramedics, and medical examiner into the house, the two women resumed hugging...and crying. They stayed there, together, arms wrapped around each other through the police questioning, and finally, the medics rolling the covered body through the kitchen.

"Wait," Shannon said. "Can I see him?"

"Honey, you don't want to do that. Trust me. I will never get that vision out of my head," Annette said. "It's better to remember him alive."

"No," Shannon said. "I need to see him."

Shannon rose and stood by the gurney. The paramedic slowly and respectfully pulled back the white sheet. Her father's face had paled. He didn't look dead, but he didn't look all that well either, especially with his blue lips. Shannon stared at him. Waiting. She didn't know what for, but she couldn't move or say anything.

The tears had stopped.

"Please," Annette said. "Please, take him away. She's just a child. She shouldn't have to see this."

The paramedics covered his face and took him away.

Shannon just stood there. Numb. Scared.

No. She was terrified.

As much as she'd dreamed of this day, she wasn't sure why she was so afraid to begin her new life.

A life free of suffering.

Free of her father's dark legacy.

She pressed her hand over her stomach.

And her child would be free, too.

CHAPTER ONE

Today marked the anniversary of the day Shannon Brendel had been given a second chance at life.

She tapped her toe to the country song playing through her speaker as she waited for the steaming bitter brew to stop dripping into her mug. Today always brought a combination of excitement, anxiety, and sheer joy. For most of her adult life, she'd done everything she could to shove the memories into a lockbox inside her mind.

But today, she embraced one small piece of her past.

So much negativity had come from her childhood. She tried hard to take all that baggage and stuff it under her bed. But the older she got, the harder it became. She needed to know that she'd done one good thing in her darkest hour.

She blew out a puff of air as butterflies filled her stomach. It was time to move forward and ask her neighbor for help.

She clutched the feather pendant dangling from her neck. Her stepmonster—no—stepmother and now best friend had given it to her shortly after her father had died, telling her it represented freedom.

Her freedom.

And what she did with the rest of her life was now her choice.

She kissed the pendant before snagging her coffee and heading outside to soak in a little morning sun as it kissed the crystal blue waters of Lake George. The second the spring air hit her body, she closed her eyes and took in a long breath, enjoying the cool breeze.

Her cottage was the last of five, each nearly identical in shape and size. A line of tall, lush trees with branches reaching across the long, curved driveway, hid the cabins from view of the main road.

The hum of a boat engine caught Shannon's attention, and she snapped her gaze toward the lake. "Oh, no," she whispered as her mug slipped from her fingers, crashing onto the wooden deck. Hot coffee singed her skin. She kicked her feet, but her stare remained on the tall mast with a line slinking down, rattling against the metal pole like a ghost gliding across the floor, rubbing its grubby fingers together, ready to capture and never let go.

"Shit. Are you okay?" Jackson Armstrong asked, seemingly appearing out of nowhere.

She swallowed the bile smacking the back of her throat as she stared at her neighbor as he bolted across the yard.

"Is that…that…?" She squeezed her eyes closed, then opened them slowly. No way could there be a thirty-five-foot Tartan sailboat moored off the end of her dock.

"Shannon." He knelt, picking up the broken ceramic pieces. "Stay still. I don't want you to cut yourself."

"Where did that come from?" She pointed toward the lake. The boat wasn't identical to the one her father had owned, and it was certainly newer, but there was no mistaking that Tartan had manufactured it.

Jackson stood, his broad shoulders blocking the morning sun but not the damn boat. It wasn't as if she hadn't seen one in the last few years. The lake was filled with them. She just never expected one to be front and center at her home.

"Isn't she pretty? I named her *Sweet Freedom*." Jackson brought his fingers to his mouth, making a kissing noise and raising his hand in the air like in a bad Italian movie.

"You've got to be kidding me," she mumbled.

"You don't like the name? I almost went with *No Sailing Around*, but Katie, my business partner, thought that was stupid."

"I agree. That's a stupid name." What was she going to do? Tell her neighbor that a boat like that represented the kind of chains that not only held a person prisoner but also held the power to destroy the remnants of what might be left of a beaten mind, body, and soul? "But having grown up around boats, you should go with something personal. Maybe something like, *Finding the Wind*, which goes hand in hand with what you do for a living."

"That's an interesting name, but as you can see, I already had *Sweet Freedom* painted on the back. And my sister came up with the name. She thinks it represents my move up here."

Shannon bit back the sarcastic laugh that threatened to escape her lips. She raised her foot to step to the grass, but Jackson lifted her into the air. "What the hell do you think you're doing?"

He set her down on the ground in front of the common picnic area between the two houses. The cool grass tickled her toes.

"There are still some slivers from your mug, and you're barefoot," he said, shaking his head.

"I like to go barefoot, and there's no need to hoist me up and drag me across the yard." She brushed at her slacks, glaring. "You could have just said, '*Be careful.*'"

Jackson raised his hands into the air. "I was trying to be a gentleman." His jeans hung low on his hips, and his untucked black T-shirt showed off his taut abs. He looked more like a Texas Ranger with his cowboy hat than a man who enjoyed sailing.

She let her gaze take in the details of the vessel's fine craftsmanship as it rolled with a few waves. There was no reason to let that boat get under her skin. She held the power, not it. "I'm sorry. I'm a little jumpy this morning."

"You don't say? I hope I'm not the one making you skittish."

"No. It's not you. It's just that my dad used to own a boat like that, and today is the anniversary of his death." She tossed in the latter only because people generally gave her their sympathies and didn't ask questions. She should feel guilty using her father's death that way.

But she didn't.

"Oh, shit. I didn't know. I'm so sorry."

"Thanks." She gave the standard response instead of asking him to jump up and down for joy and celebrate with her. "I was just startled by seeing your new toy."

She set her emotions aside and did her best to support Jackson and what seemed to be something he held dear. His boat and his life had absolutely nothing to do with her, and she needed to get over it.

"When did you get her?" Shannon asked, thankful that her voice came across as strong and steady—her insides were anything but. Mentally, she used every trick her therapist had taught her, and those she taught to *her* patients, to sedate the beast that lurked in the shadows of her mind. There would always be triggers.

And she'd always battle them.

But today, they no longer needed to control her life.

Even when the biggest trigger of all taunted her from fifty feet away.

"I bought her a couple of weeks ago. I'd love to take you out on her. Even if it's not a windy day, we could troll over to Sandy Bay or maybe up to Rogers Rock."

"I'm not a fan of sailing. Or boating, for that matter. I haven't been since my father died." She bit her tongue. Jackson had a way of making her loose-lipped. He kept his body language open, rarely crossing his legs or arms. He always made eye contact, and he seldom showed facial cues other than a relaxed jaw and a twitchy brow.

He'd make a good therapist.

"Why not?" he asked, resting his strong hand on her shoulder. His fingers squeezed gently, offering her comfort she didn't need.

She resisted the urge to shrug off his touch, but only because she didn't want to appear any ruder than she'd already been. "It just brings back too many painful memories."

"I can understand that. But maybe it's time to get back on the horse."

She coughed. "I'm not going to change my mind on this one, but I appreciate the offer."

"But you might change your mind about going out

to dinner or having drinks with me?" He rose his right brow as he tipped his hat. "I told you, I'm a persistent kind of guy."

The corners of her mouth tugged upward into an involuntary smile. The man wouldn't give up, no matter how many times she said no. And at this point, she wasn't sure why she continued turning him down.

He was kind.

Considerate as he always carried her groceries.

Shoveled the snow when it got out of hand.

And he was handsome.

Maybe it was time to say yes.

He twisted a piece of her hair between his fingers. "You got your hair cut."

She pushed a strand behind her ear, a little dumbfounded that he noticed. "I needed a change."

He pointed to his forehead. "I like the bang thing. And shoulder-length fits your face."

"Are you trying to use flattery to get me to go out with you?" With most men, flirting felt as stiff and phony as cheap leather sticking to the back side of her legs on a hot summer day. With Jackson, the kind words coated her body with a soft, foamy lather that, when washed away, still lingered with a refreshing tingle.

"Can't blame a guy for trying."

"I am impressed you noticed," she said. "I suppose I should give you points for that."

He shrugged. "I have five sisters."

"Ah, that explains a lot," she said with a laugh.

"What's that supposed to mean?" He leaned against the railing, folding one arm across his chest, while sipping his coffee.

It was the first time she'd noticed any hint of annoyance in his tone and body language.

Stop sizing him up. He's your neighbor, not a client.

"Your taste in furniture, for one." She pointed to his front door. "I mean, I've never met a bachelor who has a place that looks like it should be the centerfold for *Lake Living*. It looks like you had it staged with how the leather sofa sits a few inches from the back wall and the matching chair at a ninety-degree angle in the corner by the stairs. And don't get me started on the picture over the couch. A man would not pick out an authentic image of the lake. No, he would have picked out dogs fishing or some such crazy thing."

"You're picking on me for having good taste?" He dropped his hand to his side and grinned.

"Oh, good grief. No." She shook her head. "It's just that the first time I walked into your house, I thought I entered a showroom. Or worse, my mother's living room, where nothing can be touched without wearing gloves."

"My sisters did the whole thing. I just unloaded the crap off the U-Haul using my brute strength and put it where they told me."

"For some reason, I think you had a lot of say in the décor."

"A little. I mean, one of my sisters is an interior decorator, and it's rubbed off on me."

"That's cute. Are you all close?"

His smile widened, and his dark eyes sparkled like the moon dancing on the waters below. "Actually, we are. But they all live in Delaware, where I'm originally from. I'm hoping to get them up here with their families for the Fourth of July. It would be a lot of fun. My sisters are all pretty loud and very protective of me."

"Really? Isn't it the brother who is supposed to defend their sisters' honor?"

"I'm the baby."

Laughter floated easily from her throat. She enjoyed Jackson way more than she should. For the last year, she'd admired him from a distance, but she wouldn't let herself get too close. He was the kind of man who could break through her carefully crafted defenses, and she wasn't ready to get involved with anyone.

Not yet.

Not until she knew that she'd given her little girl a better a life.

Since her father died, she hadn't had much time for dating. Getting her PhD had been one hell of a ride. She still didn't have time for a man, but she could use a friend. "The youngest of six and the only boy. Perhaps we should talk about that and how it's affected your adult life."

"Don't start your therapy stuff with me." He pointed to the broken mug on the table. "Can I get you a refill?"

"I was hoping to see you this morning. I have something I need to talk to you about."

"That sounds ominous." Jackson had a rugged look about him. The deepening wrinkles around his eyes indicated a man who had seen a few things in his life. She figured him to be in his late thirties or very early forties—not that much older than her. Not that it mattered.

He wasn't too tall, maybe five-ten. And he had a kind heart and didn't mind showing it. If she were any other woman, she'd probably be falling at his feet.

Instead, she just drooled over him in private.

"I'll be right back. I just put a fresh pot on," he said.

She stared at the side of his house, avoiding the lake and the boat. She had overreacted, but it wouldn't be easy seeing a constant reminder of what her father had done to her or what she'd been forced to give up.

"Here you go." Jackson handed her a cup. The bitter aroma filled her nose like pure, unsweetened cocoa. "Are you free for dinner tonight?"

She laughed. "I'm actually having dinner with my stepmother, but maybe we can have a drink after."

"Are you actually agreeing to a date?" he asked with wide eyes and a big, goofy smile.

The man was too cute for his own good.

"Not a date. Just a drink with a friend. Say around nine? Right here? We can build a fire."

"Sounds great to me." He raised his mug.

"Can I ask you a work-related question?"

"Sure," Jackson said.

"Do you ever take on cases for friends?"

"All the time. Why?"

She stole a peek at the sailboat. That night had changed her life in more ways than one. "I'd like to hire you."

"For?" He set his coffee on the railing, easing closer, leaving his arms dangling at his sides.

He must have taken a ton of psychology courses because he knew exactly how to put someone at ease. Anyone would bare their soul to this man and not even know they were doing it.

She let out a puff of air. The only person she'd ever spoken to about her daughter had been Annette. Even her mother couldn't bear to hear about it, always telling Shannon that she'd been a horrible teenager and to pray for forgiveness.

"Two things, actually. I don't like doing this, but a...a friend of mine missed a lunch date on Friday, and I haven't been able to reach her all weekend. She's never done that, and I'm a little worried. Could I trouble you to just check on her or something? I don't mind paying you."

"I can do that," he said, but the way he tilted his head indicated that he wasn't buying the friend part.

Shit. She could get fired for that one.

"I'm just concerned, and I want to know she's okay."

"You just want me to get a visual? Or do you need me to contact her?"

Shannon looked at the sky for an answer. Deep down in the pit of her stomach, she knew that something wasn't right with Belinda, and she couldn't let it go. "Just a visual. Her name is Belinda Montgomery, and she—"

"Name is all I need. If I want more, I'll call," he said.

"Thanks."

"No problem. And no need to pay me. Now, what's the second?"

"This one is a little bit more detailed, and I'll insist on compensating you for your time." She reached for her pendant, running her finger up and down the feathered sides. Not a day went by that she didn't wear the necklace. It drove her mother crazy, but only because of where it had come from and the fact that Shannon still had a relationship with her father's second wife.

"If it makes you feel more comfortable, your case will be confidential. The only other person who will know the details, or your name, will be Katie, my partner."

"I can't say that makes me feel better. This is pretty personal and not easy for me." But she wasn't going to turn back now. She just needed a few deep breaths. In through the nose and out through the mouth. Slow and controlled. "I want to find the child I gave up for adoption." Her fingers trembled over the silver jewelry dangling from her neck. Her gaze darted toward the parking area, focusing on Jackson's shiny pickup truck. A diesel. It had rumbled many a late night, loud and proud. But it always calmed her nerves, even when it woke her up.

Jackson was one of the few men who always made her feel safe.

"You want me to find the kid you gave up?" Jackson's tone had an edge she'd only heard when he got upset with the lawn guy for ruining his rose bush. Jackson hadn't ever yelled at the groundskeeper, but the anger lacing his words was more terrifying than any screaming match could be.

Shannon swallowed the thick lump in her throat. This was turning out to be harder than she'd thought. Her fears over being judged ran wild, and she knew that she read too much into Jackson's attitude. "This may sound odd, but I just want to know if she's okay. That she was placed in a good home."

He raked a hand through his long hair. "I'm sorry. I'm going to have to say no. I don't do adoption cases under any circumstances." He turned his back and leaned against the deck with his arms folded across his chest.

Closed-off. And the tension that filled the air nearly choked her. The therapist in her wanted to ask probing questions to tackle the problem at hand. To figure out why adoption cases were a trigger for him. But she reminded herself that he wasn't her client, and this was about her finding her daughter and getting some closure for her past.

"Why not?" she asked. The thumping of her heart roared in her head. "I would think you'd get a lot of cases like this in your line of work." She didn't care what his issues were, only why he didn't want to do her a favor.

Or at the very least, take her money.

"And I always turn them away. It's nothing personal—"

"Like hell." She took him by the shoulder and yanked until his body twisted. She caught his gaze and gasped at the judgment staring back at her. "This is very personal to me, and you're not only saying no—which, okay, you have that right—but you're also condemning me and my decision, and that's not fair. You don't know my history. Or anything about why I might have been completely incapable of raising a child at sixteen."

He let out a long breath, nodding as if he understood. But he didn't. How could he? "Please understand, I'm not judging what you did. I do, however, have a problem with what you're asking me to do."

"I think you owe me the reason why, at least," she said under her breath. For years, she'd let her mother pretend that Shannon had never had a baby. She allowed the shame her mother felt to become hers. Not anymore. And she'd be damned if she would let Jackson—or anyone for that matter—make her feel shitty for one of the most difficult decisions she'd ever had to make.

"Do you want the truth?" he asked, glancing over his shoulder, his dark orbs conveying a resolve that could only mask a crushing pain. She saw it every day in the eyes of the patients she treated.

The same look stared back at her every morning.

And today, she could see it cut deep into Jackson's psychological make-up. Her pulse steadied as she braced herself for his explanation. "I expect nothing less from you," she said.

"You might not like what I have to say."

"I don't like what you've said so far, so I don't think you're going to make it worse. At least maybe I'll understand and respect your decision."

"I don't think it's right for birth parents to insert themselves into the lives of the children they gave up. Maybe if it were the other way around, and the child wanted to know... But even then, I'd still decline the case. I've seen what it can do to families."

"But you'll spy on a woman because her husband thinks she's cheating." She smoothed her hands down her slacks.

"You're right. I will," he said with a steely tone. "I'm not the only private investigator in town. I can recommend someone who will do an excellent job. In the meantime, I'm still happy to check in on your friend." He downed his coffee in one gulp. "I'll text you contact information for a buddy of mine. I send him a lot of cases like this. He's good, and he'll be discreet. I'm really sorry, but it would be like asking you to perform brain surgery just because you have a PhD. It's not your specialty."

She opened her mouth and snapped it shut three times. His specialty was finding people. Said so right on his business card that he'd given her when they first met. She had half a mind to call him on his bullshit, but the sudden screeching of tires spinning on the pavement of the road above caught her attention.

A van nearly missed a vehicle at a standstill at the top of their driveway.

"Stupid place to park a car." Jackson flipped his mug, tossing the last few drops of the liquid to the grass. "Do you happen to know the owner of that vehicle?"

She stared at a light blue sedan. "I don't think so." She shook her head. "But the first cabin on the hill isn't rented this year, that I know of. Maybe it's someone looking into it."

"Third morning in a row that I've noticed. But it's never there before I go to bed at night."

"Do you think it's something we should be worried about?" she asked.

"I'm probably being paranoid. I should really get going." He tipped his hat.

"I'll see you tonight at nine."

"I know you've got plans with family, so take your time. We can do drinks another night."

"Are you canceling on me because I had a baby when I was a young girl and gave her up?" She drew her lips into a tight line, breathing in through her nose and exhaling with purpose. It wouldn't be the first time a man had taken offense to her choice.

Or maybe it was because she'd had sex at such a young age. Imagine if he knew the truth. That would blow his mind into a million tiny pieces.

"It's not that. I just think with it being the anniversary of your father's death and being around your family, it might be best if we do it another night."

"I don't need you to think for me." She shoved the mug at his chest. "Thanks for the coffee." She turned on her heel and stomped into her house, slamming the door.

She didn't need Jackson to find her daughter.

She didn't need him to have a drink with her.

Hell, she didn't need him one damn bit.

Her phone buzzed.

She glanced at her mother's name flashing across the screen. "Sorry, Mom, I'm not dealing with your drama today."

————

Jackson took off his sunglasses, slipped them into his front pocket, and stared across the parking lot at the local bank in the middle of Saratoga Springs, about twenty-five minutes south of the village of Lake George.

He shouldn't have been so harsh with his response to Shannon's request. He certainly could have declined in a way that didn't make him come off like a judgmental asshole. He respected the fact that she'd been brave enough to have a child at sixteen and give it up for adoption.

That had been the only good thing his birth mother had done, and he wished she'd left well enough alone.

"You look constipated. And whenever you scrunch your forehead like that, something is bothering you." Katie said. "Now, lay it on me."

"I just have a lot on my mind. Don't forget to send the check to the painters. They really did a great job."

"You're such a girl," Katie said. "Your smooth, chocolate-whatever paint isn't going to act as some kind of truth serum, so our clients tell us why they really hired us. We don't need to be their therapist, and we certainly don't need to know all the sorted details of their lives. We just need the work, and we're the best at finding things."

"We are. And it was my sister who picked out the color. You have to admit, the office looks so much better."

"And that's necessary because we spend so much time there," she said with all the snark she was notorious for. Katie tended to hide behind angst. He'd gotten used to it and found it endearing, but it didn't have that effect on most people.

"Hey. When we aren't on a stakeout, we might as well enjoy our surroundings."

"Whatever makes you happy," she said.

He did his best to keep his mind on the task at hand and not how he needed to apologize to Shannon.

Or how he wanted to kiss her.

And not just once.

And not only on the lips.

Shannon had been driving him crazy for months. And while she always politely declined his advances, she continued to passively flirt—if there was such a thing. She'd give him a slight smile with a wave, and if he looked close enough, he could see a mischievous twinkle in her eye. A few times, when the temperatures rose above fifty, regardless of the season, they shared in-depth conversations about topics in the news. She had to be one of the most insightful women he'd ever met. Every morning, he checked the weather, hoping it was warm enough so he might be able to catch her hanging outside, sipping her coffee. He couldn't imagine a better way to start his day.

Katie thumbed through the file they had compiled this morning. "According to our client, Miss Belinda Montgomery should be in the bank."

"But she's not." Jackson pulled out the piece of paper from his pocket with the license plate of the sedan that had been parked by his house and set it on the dashboard. "Don't you think it's weird that someone hired us to find this girl yesterday evening, and then this morning, my neighbor asked me to check in on her?"

"What did you tell the pretty doctor?"

"Nothing, just that I'd check up on her *friend*."

"No such thing as coincidences." Katie tilted her head. "Is Belinda Dr. Brendel's patient?"

"She didn't say. But I'd say that's a good guess. Once I heard the name, I knew it could get awkward, so I just told her I'd get a visual, which is all she wanted anyway."

"Belinda's a recovering addict, along with her roommate. That is just the kind of thing the doctor specializes in."

Janice Hargrove, Belinda's roommate, had been concerned that her friend might have relapsed. Jackson had to agree. "So, our missing girl is probably off filling her nose full of coke somewhere," Jackson said. He knew all too well that addicts, no matter how many times they professed that they'd changed, used again. It was only a matter of time.

He'd given his birth mother a couple of second chances, and she'd snorted all the money he'd lent her. He'd smartened up when she asked him for a kidney. He never wished the woman dead, but she'd died two years after she found a kidney donor—of a drug overdose. His muscles tightened as he thought of all the people who could have used that kidney and wouldn't have taken it for granted.

But his birth mother had been a selfish woman, never thinking about anyone but herself, except for the day she'd dropped him off at a fire station, where his adoptive...no, his *real* father had been working.

"People can and do kick the habit, you know."

"For maybe five minutes," Jackson said as he opened the door. The crisp air smacked his skin, but summer was well on its way, and so was the insanity that came with living in a tourist town. "People don't change that much." When his birth mother had first come into his life, he experimented with drugs, looking for her approval. He'd gotten lost in the insanity of the world, but thanks to his family, he'd gotten back on the straight and narrow.

But he hadn't been an addict. He hadn't developed a physical or emotional need for the chemical.

He had, however, developed that need for his birth mother. In a way, she'd become his drug of choice. He wondered if he'd still allow her in and out of his life had she not ripped his heart from his chest and fed it to the wolves.

"You're the most optimistic person I know, except with this particular subject. Well, this and marriage, but I know why you're not a fan of wedded bliss. But why don't you think people can change their stripes?" Katie took off her hat, fiddled with her ponytail, and then leapt from the Jeep, landing perfectly in her three-inch heels, which didn't go with her torn-up pants. He couldn't even tell if they were sweats, fatigues, or maybe a pair of mangled slacks.

"Because I've seen it time and time again. Only five percent of those who kick the habit stay the course for life. That's a fact."

"That's a statistic, and it could be wrong." Katie adjusted her baseball cap, showing off her French manicure. She took long strides, her heels clicking against the pavement. It amazed him that the woman didn't fall on her face half the time.

They continued walking toward the bank's entrance. The sun beat down on the dark pavement. It would hit sixty-five by noon. He opened the door, and they entered the institution. It was a relatively small bank. Three tellers and a drive-thru window to the right of the doors. To the left was a welcome desk, a white-haired woman sitting behind it with a big smile. "May I help you?" she asked.

"We'd like to speak to Miss Montgomery," Katie said with a return smile.

"I'm sorry, she's not here today. Can someone else help you?"

"May we speak with her boss?" Katie asked.

"One moment please," the woman said, then turned her chair and slowly lowered herself. She took a few steps before she disappeared behind a wall to what appeared to be four offices, cubical style.

Jackson and Katie waited patiently for about five

minutes before the elderly woman reappeared. "Ms. Timms will see you now." She waved them in.

Jackson followed Katie into the office. He almost always let her take the lead. A short, heavyset, middle-aged woman who couldn't be taller than five feet greeted them. She stood behind her desk with an extended hand. "I am Lisa Timms, the bank manager. What can I help you with today?"

"Ms. Timms. My name is Jackson Armstrong, and this is Katie Bateman," Jackson started. "We don't want to alarm you, but we are private investigators and are looking for Belinda Montgomery."

Ms. Timms sat down and folded her hands on the desk. She looked him directly in the eye when she spoke. "I cannot discuss my employees with you. I am sorry."

"Can you at least tell us when you last spoke to Miss Montgomery?" Katie asked in her best feminine voice, the one she thought other women related to. In reality, they didn't.

"Thursday." Ms. Timms frowned. "If something has happened and I need to speak to the police or something, then I would be more than happy to cooperate with them."

Katie leaned forward, resting her hand on the desk. Her smile seemed forced, but then again, he knew her too well. Others didn't have his insight. "We don't mean to alarm you, ma'am. A friend of Miss Montgomery's is concerned because she has not heard from her in a while."

Ms. Timms let out a long breath. "Well, I can tell you that Miss Montgomery requested a few days off. She's an excellent employee and has never taken a sick day, so I gave her the personal time. I'm sure it's just a misunderstanding." Now, it was Ms. Timms' turn to lean in. "Between you and me." Ms. Timms looked about the office before focusing her attention on Katie. "If this is her roommate, I know they had somewhat of an argument. So maybe Miss Montgomery just needed a little space."

"Really," Jackson said. "Can you elaborate?" He didn't have the same charm as Katie did, but women generally responded to him just the same.

"No." Ms. Timms leaned back in her chair and shook her head. "I would be gossiping and talking out of turn. I've already said too much, but I thought you should know you could be on a wild goose chase. I'm sure she's just having a romantic getaway."

"Romantic?" Jackson questioned, a bit dismayed that his charm hadn't gotten more from the woman.

"Oh, dear. Me and my big mouth." Ms. Timms fanned herself.

"When is Miss Montgomery due back to work?" Katie asked.

"In two days," Ms. Timms said.

"So...Wednesday," Jackson clarified.

"Shall I have her give you a call when she returns?"

Ms. Timms asked as she leaned back and folded her arms across her chest in a closed-off manner.

Jackson knew when to call it quits. He stood and pulled out a business card, placing it face-up on the desk. "Yes, please do."

"Thank you for your time," Katie said, glancing up at him with an evil stare.

She liked to be in control. All the time. She always wanted to call the shots, and for the most part, she was always on point. But sometimes, she pushed too hard. This would be one of those times.

They made their way back outside, where the temperature had already risen at least five degrees.

Katie's temp probably exceeded that of a hot tub. "You excused us a little too early."

"She wasn't going to give us more. Besides, she doesn't know any more," he said.

"You don't know that."

Jackson wasn't about to continue down this road. "If Belinda requested time off from the bank, I think she would have canceled and rescheduled her visit with Shannon."

"When was her appointment?"

"Last Friday. Which means, she knew she wouldn't be around when she asked for the time off. So, again, it doesn't make sense for her to blow off the appointment." Jackson got in the Jeep and grabbed the piece of paper he'd left on the dashboard.

"I don't know. A lot of people forget about doctor

appointments or feel guilty about canceling, so they just don't go."

"Maybe." He pulled his iPad from the backseat, opened email, and sent the license plate number to a cop friend.

"What are you doing?" Katie fired up the Jeep. It sputtered, then let out a loud roar as she pressed on the gas.

"You need a new muffler," he said.

"You haven't answered my question."

"Having a friend check a license plate number." He folded the iPad case closed and returned it to the backseat. "I meant to do it earlier. A car's been at the top of my driveway for three mornings in a row."

"That's weird," Katie said. "Why do you think it's suspicious, other than it not being a safe place to park?"

"Have you ever known me to be anything *but* guarded?" he said. Shannon was most likely right about it being someone looking into renting one of the cottages. "I've got a weird vibe about this Belinda Montgomery case."

"So do I." Katie got back onto the Northway, headed toward Lake George. "I suspect Ms. Timms is more of a gossip, so I think we can push her if we have to."

"I agree." Jackson grabbed hold of the holy-shit bar. "When are you going to learn this Jeep is not a race car?"

"The moment you stop caring about decorating."

"Har, har," he said, glancing at the speedometer.

"Geez, lucky for you, your boyfriend is an assistant district attorney."

"He's not my boyfriend," she said with venom. "Janice said they had a fight on Friday about how Belinda hadn't cleaned up her dirty dishes. But, seriously, that's not a reason to disappear for days without a word."

"Which is why I think she fell off the wagon."

"You really need to start giving people the benefit of the doubt," Katie said. "But in this case, I have to agree. Which is why you need to talk to that doctor neighbor of yours."

"She's not going to be able to give us any insight." Jackson continued gripping the bar above his head as Katie weaved in and out of traffic. "Seriously, you're going to get a ticket."

She pointed to the sticker on her windshield. "I have friends in high places, and you need to use that charm you swear you have on Shannon. We need to know where to look. Janice didn't know Belinda until after rehab, so she doesn't know much about her past. I'm sure her shrink will know more."

"She's not a shrink; she's a therapist."

"Whatever. Just promise me you will talk to her."

"I will, but I'm going to be honest with her about why I want to know." And he'd apologize, too.

Katie shook her head. "Then she's going to clam up on us, protecting her client."

"Ah, ye of little faith. You underestimate my ability to charm women."

Katie laughed. Loudly. "You do know that most women think you're gay after spending about five minutes with you, right? Really, you shouldn't let on all you know about decorating and fashion and all that girly stuff. We're never going to get you a woman."

It was his turn to laugh, and he tossed in a flick of his hair for good measure. "First, I've already landed one woman."

"Who turned out to be a bitch."

That cut his laugh short. "This, coming from a woman who doesn't even own a dress, much less a decent pair of slacks. Seriously, no wonder you're still single."

"Oh, bite me."

"Nice mouth."

"Yeah, yeah," she said, adjusting her baseball cap as she slowed down to go through the EZPass lane. "Just talk to the good old doctor. I'm going to drop you off at the office and tell Jessica she needs to file an official missing person's case. At least that way, I can get some of our friends down there to help me out with some intel."

"Good tax dollars at work. Get the PI to do all the grunt labor."

"Hey, we're getting paid on this one, so bite your tongue."

"True," he said just as they pulled into the office

parking lot, situated behind the main drag of Lake George and right behind Gunners, a local watering hole. It was a quiet town, and most of their work was little things: divorce cases, runaway teens. Every once in a while, they got a case from Saratoga—like this one. Or from Albany. But for the most part, his life was quiet and calm.

Just the way he wanted it.

CHAPTER TWO

Shannon pulled open her office door and gasped. The last person she ever expected to see sitting in her waiting room was her mother.

Melinda Cartwright had once said she'd never be caught dead in a therapist's office, even if that office belonged to her daughter. Psychologists and psychiatrists were for the weak and mentally unstable—the truly sick and unsavory people of the world. Those twisted minds that even God's salvation couldn't mend.

"Hello, Mother."

"I hate it when you call me that." Her mom stood with all the style and grace expected of the queen. "I need to—"

"I'll be with you in about fifteen minutes." Shannon held out her hand.

Her mother didn't like to wait for anyone, and given how she drew her lips into a tight line, she wasn't happy to have been dismissed. Too bad. Shannon wasn't about to interrupt a client's session because her mother thought the world centered around her.

"It will only take—"

"Excuse me." Shannon turned her back and faced her client's father. "Please, come inside," she said to Greg Mallory, who had been sitting quietly in the corner.

His gaze darted between the two women before he rushed through the doorway.

"Fifteen minutes, Mother." Shannon didn't wait for a response, but she did take in a deep, calming breath. If someone had died or had been injured, her mom would have barged right through her office door with no regard for the patient's privacy. Whatever her mother needed, it could wait.

"Please. Make yourself comfortable." Shannon sat in her gray-blue wingback chair, making sure she had her pen and pad. She needed something to fiddle with, while her mother probably paced a hole in her waiting room carpet. "Lilly and I thought it would be good for you to join us for a few minutes."

"Is something wrong?" Greg asked. He'd taken the spot next to his daughter, but when he got too close, she curled up into a ball, hugging her knees.

Greg let out a long sigh, his shoulders hunched in defeat.

"Lilly and I were talking about how things have been going since she moved into your house."

"It's been a major adjustment for all of us," he admitted.

"I can only imagine." Shannon diverted her gaze to the clock on the wall. "I suggested to Lilly that perhaps we could schedule some family sessions. If you are agreeable."

"I am," Greg said, rubbing his hands up and down his legs. "I was going to ask if maybe I could come and talk with you, as well. I'm trying. I really am. I want to make this work."

"Trying too hard," Lilly muttered. "So hard, I can tell you don't want me there."

"That's not true." Greg inched closer, but he didn't touch her.

Shannon suspected that Lilly would probably react negatively to the intimacy, and Greg seemed to be smart enough not to force his need to hold and comfort his daughter. They barely knew each other since Lilly's mother had kept Lilly from her father for most of her life. He hadn't even known she existed until she was seven years old.

"You look at me like I've ruined your life." Lilly pulled her hoodie over her head.

"You haven't ruined anything. None of this is your fault."

Shannon stole a second glance at the time. Thankfully, this wasn't the first time Lilly and her father had had this conversation. But so far, they never got past the blame game.

Shannon jotted a few squiggly lines on her pad. No words. Just getting out her anxiety over who sat in the waiting room. She needed to focus on her client. "Lilly. Can you ask your father what you mentioned to me?"

The girl nodded, swiping at her cheeks and setting her feet on the floor.

"What is it, Lilly?" Greg closed the gap. This time, he rested his hand on her shoulder. It wasn't an intimate gesture, but it was physical contact.

"Are you afraid of me? Do you think I'll hurt my little brother or sister?"

Greg shook his head. "God, sweetie. No. What makes you think that?"

"You never leave me alone with them, and Julie won't let me babysit."

"We've told you why. Until you stop"—Greg tapped her forearm—"hurting yourself, and I know you're not still cutting. I worry that something will trigger that need when you are with them. And you're still smoking, something I won't have in my house. I hate that you hurt yourself, and I wish I knew what to do to help you, but we need rules. Most of which, you laid out for yourself before moving in."

"I know. But you're not going to trust me no matter what I do." Lilly pulled her sleeves down over her hands.

"I trust that you love your siblings. What I don't trust is that you're ready for the responsibility."

"This will all take time. It's only been a couple of

weeks since we left the courtroom, and you left the facility," Shannon said. "But if you stick with our plan, I think things will change."

"What plan?" Greg asked.

"I told the doc I'd start writing in a journal when I felt the urge. Or I'd talk to you—which is what she prefers." Lilly pointed toward Shannon.

"I prefer it, too," Greg said. "I don't judge you, sweetie. I just want it to stop."

"That's why I asked you here. I think it's a good idea for your wife to come in, as well," Shannon interjected.

Greg nodded. "I know Julie would be happy to. All we want is for Lilly to get better. For all of us to heal." He wiped his face, his eyes filled with tears. "I should have known what was going on at her mother's."

"Greg. Don't go down the *should-have* road. It won't help you or your family. We need to focus on the positive and what we can do today to help Lilly. We spoke at length about the triggers for cutting, and we've developed coping mechanisms Lilly can use. We've discussed the more she withdraws from you, the worse it gets. So, you and Julie need to help pull her back in. It's not going to change overnight, but we're on the right track." Shannon stood to keep herself from tapping her foot on the floor. "I hate to do this, but our time is up for today. Why don't you look at your schedule, and we can set up a couple of sessions together? Perhaps I can meet alone with you and your wife, too."

"I'll call you later today to schedule something.

Thanks, doc." Greg took his daughter by the hand and pulled her close to his side, kissing the top of her head.

Lilly didn't shove him away or cringe.

That was progress.

"We'll do whatever it takes," Greg continued.

Shannon nodded. "Lilly? How does this all sound to you?"

"It sounds good." Lilly blinked, showing off her blue eyes that reminded Shannon of the sky on the sunniest of days. A world of hurt still filled them, but today, they also showed the promise of hope.

Hope that today things will be different.

Shannon held the door for her client and her father. She smiled sweetly, squeezing Lilly's arm as she walked through the door.

Counting to ten, Shannon reminded herself that being kind didn't make her a pushover.

That said, she needed to keep her boundaries firmly in place when it came to *her* family.

"Mother," Shannon said, turning her back and heading into the office once more. She stood in front of the counter where she kept her Keurig, not offering her mother a cup. "What brings you by?" She took a long, slow sip of her coffee, letting the liquid burn as it flowed down her throat.

"You look like you've put on a couple of pounds. Maybe it's the haircut, which ages you. At thirty-five, that's the last thing you want to do." Melinda

Cartwright had an opinion for everything, and she was always right, no matter what.

"I don't weigh myself, so I wouldn't know."

"Of course, you don't. But you should. That way, you'd know, and you could keep a handle on it," her mother said with a dismissive wave of her hand. "I'm surprised by how nice this place is." She strolled into the office with her nose in the air and judgment in her glare. "But it could use some pictures. Maybe you should put a couple of family photos on your desk. We'll get some good ones at the wedding."

"Mom," Shannon said. "I've got another patient coming shortly. What do you need?"

"Oh, and you should really hang the picture of your father, you, your uncle, and your grandparents right up there." She pointed to the wall over the couch and moved closer. "You still have that picture, don't you?"

Shannon didn't have a single picture of her father. Not one. And her mother knew it. "Mom, I don't—"

"Hard to believe it's been eighteen years since your father died. I miss him." Her mother pulled a tissue out of her bag and dabbed her perfectly made-up eyes. The lids were covered in a stylish light purple with a bit of sparkle. Her thick eyelashes blinked widely over her soft blue eyes.

Melinda always looked as if she were ready to walk the red carpet. Her bouncy brown curls flowed over her shoulders. Not a single hair out of place, and absolutely no frizz. Not even on the most humid days in the summer. Today, her lips looked a little too full, especially when she talked. Perhaps she'd just had her collagen injections. Her designer pantsuit clung to her toned body she'd paid a small fortune for, between liposuction and a personal trainer.

And more surgeries.

If Shannon were asked to describe her mother, in all honesty, she would say that Melinda Cartwright was the original authentic phony.

"We both know Dad wasn't a stand-up guy, so why do you insist on pretending he was? Have you forgotten the things he did to you? To *me*?" It really wasn't overly smart to goad her mother, but it was the anniversary of Shannon's new life, and there was no way in hell she would let Mommy Dearest mess with that.

Her mother gave her a scathing glare. "I have forgiven him. You should, too. He's dead. Show some respect. He was your damned father, whether you like it or not." Her mother stuffed the tissue into her purse and drew her fat lips into a tight line. "I didn't come here to argue over your inability to forgive and forget."

Shannon wanted to jump all over that one but chose not to. "Why *did* you stop by this morning?"

"It's Tara. Her boyfriend broke up with her. I have half a mind to go to his house and talk some sense into that young man. Or maybe I should go straight to his father. But then I figured out a better way to deal with the problem."

"Don't meddle in her life," Shannon said, knowing the warning would fall on deaf ears. "You can't make Kevin and Tara get back together. It's up to them." And if the world would just leave the two of them alone, they'd likely figure out just how much they loved each other. *If* they had actually called it quits. The last time this happened, all the two love birds had was a little spat, and Shannon's mother had simply overreacted, as she always did.

"Oh, they will get back together. You can count on that."

"Maybe, but you need to stay out of it." Shannon made a mental note to call her half-sister. Not to interfere, but to lend an ear if needed.

"All they need is a little help. And that's where you come in."

Shannon put up her hands defensively. "Oh, no. I'm not getting involved in one of your schemes. The last times you did that, Tara didn't speak to me for a week."

"I'm doing nothing of the sort, and if you would stop interrupting me like a child and let me finish, you'd see that." Melinda placed her hands on her hips and scowled. "I just want to fake fix up Tara. Maybe with that cute neighbor of yours, just to make Kevin jealous."

"Are you kidding?" Shannon stared at her mother. She shouldn't be shocked, but this was over the top, even for her mom. "First off, my neighbor is much older than Tara, and I wouldn't put him in the middle of your game."

"What? Are you saying your sister isn't good enough for him?"

"That's not the point. You'd be using him, and that's not right."

Melinda's eyes teared. How the woman did that on command had always remained a mystery. "I ask you to do one little favor for your sister to make her happy, and you refuse. You care nothing for anyone but yourself. You can't even respect your father's memory by having a picture of him in your office."

"I don't want anything personal in my office," Shannon said with a huff. She didn't owe her mother any explanation, yet she found herself reverting to old behaviors.

"Every doctor has something personal in their office. It's how they relate to their patients," her mother said as if she were the expert. "But since you're not ever going to listen to your mother, let's get back to your neighbor. He's a private investigator or something, right? I bet he sees Kevin's father every so often. I'm sure he's the investigator the law firm uses."

Shannon rolled her eyes. "Yeah. Actually, he is a PI. And I've hired him."

"For what?" Her mother dropped her hands to her sides and narrowed her eyes into tiny slits, but they were still open enough to shoot a few daggers in Shannon's direction.

"You know why," Shannon said with a tight fist.

Her mother gasped.

Shannon swallowed the fear that beat through her heart. Exposing her emotions to her mother had proven dangerous in the past.

"Why would you do that?" Melinda whispered, looking around. "It's best to leave dirty little secrets in the closet. Not even your stepfather knows what you did."

"It's not a dirty secret, and he knows; he just doesn't want to start a fight with you," Shannon muttered. Though she had lived nearly decades of her life mired in shame for what had happened and what she'd done. Not a day went by that she hadn't wondered what her daughter had become. If good, loving parents had raised her.

Not the freakshow that Shannon had been subjected to.

"It's not something this family discusses. Ever. And I won't have it. Tell your neighbor you made a mistake." Her mother fanned her face as if to dry her fake tears. "You probably ruined this for Tara, but I'd like you to introduce them anyway. See how it plays out."

Shannon heard the outside door to her office open. "Mom," she said in a soft voice, "look, I believe Jackson has a girlfriend. I see someone over there all the time, so I don't think that is the answer. Just let Tara and Kevin figure things out on their own. She's a smart girl." Shannon placed her hand on her mother's elbow. "I'm sorry, but I've really got to go."

"Right. You have sick people to fix," her mother said sarcastically. "Don't forget the bridesmaid dress fitting this Saturday. I expect you to be there on time and with a smile on your face. You're lucky that Bonnie even asked you to be in the wedding, considering how you feel about her fiancé."

"I don't dislike Fred. It's just weird that I dated him, and now she's marrying him."

"Well. Don't be late."

"I will be there. I promise," Shannon said, guiding her mother to the door, ignoring the desire to tell her to take a flying leap into the lake. She had tried to cut her mother out of her life once, but that had made it more difficult to maintain a relationship with her stepfather and her half-sister—two people she loved deeply and wanted in her life. For the most part, she and her mother had little contact, but this wedding had forced them to see each other more than at the usual family holiday gatherings. Once it was over, her mother would go back to ignoring Shannon.

And Shannon would go back to her peaceful life.

———

Shannon entered the Boardwalk Restaurant, trying to shake off the tension in her neck and shoulders. The day had been long and hard, and there was still no word from her patient, Belinda. But what had her muscles tied up in knots had been the car in the parking lot. It looked identical to the one that had been parked at the top of her driveway.

The same one Jackson had pointed out.

She'd taken a picture of the license plate with her phone and texted it to Jackson. He responded immediately, letting her know he'd already taken the number, and then he reminded her not to walk to her car by herself.

But nothing about meeting for a drink after her dinner, and Shannon wasn't sure how she felt about that. She wasn't thinking about it so much because dating him was such a high priority, but because she resented the way his demeanor had changed the second she'd revealed a smidgeon of data about her past.

However, she'd looked forward to this meal all day, and she'd be damned if she let anything stand in her way of enjoying it now.

That said, coming into this place always caused her a bit of concern. She sucked in a deep breath, scanning the bar area, checking out every middle-aged man with graying hair but doing her best to avoid eye contact.

"Boo!"

Shannon jumped, nearly falling over. She clutched her feather pendant. "Jesus, Cameron. You scared the shit out of me."

"What are best friends for if not to make you pee

your pants?" Cameron looped her arm over Shannon's shoulder. "How are you holding up?"

"Other than my mother showing up at my office, I'm good." Shannon shook out her hands. In the year she'd lived here, and in the eighteen years she'd been coming to celebrate her father's death, she'd never once come across a man she'd known in the past, but that didn't mean they weren't still lurking in the shadows.

"She didn't." Cameron's voice screeched over the country music playing in the background. "I remember when we graduated from college, how mortified she was when you let her know you'd be going for a PhD in psychology. And of all the days for her to show up... Does she even remember what today is?"

"Oh, she remembers. And she wears it on her chest like some sort of medal. But she didn't come by to commiserate."

"Right, because you both really miss that bastard. So, why *did* she show up?"

"Tara and her boyfriend broke up again. I'm sure it had to do with my mother's meddling." Shannon wove her way through the crowd toward the bar. "Where's Peter?"

"Right behind you," Peter said, making her jump again.

"Shit. The two of you really need to stop sneaking up on me."

"Shannon," Annette called from the front of the restaurant. Now there was a woman who was not only

55

loud but also commanded attention with her personality. Her looks hadn't changed much in the last eighteen years, but the woman had.

"Doesn't your stepmother know that bright blue eyeshadow and big hair went out of style back in the eighties?" Cameron whispered.

Shannon laughed. "She's been slowly waiting for it to come back in style."

"Oh, my God. Shouldn't the two of you still be on your honeymoon?" Annette asked as she yanked Cameron in for a big hug, kissing her cheeks, leaving bright red lipstick on her skin.

Annette had an uncanny way of spreading joy and sunshine. Her life had been hard, even before she met and married Shannon's father, but she'd managed to pick up the pieces. And when she put a smile on her face, she put one on everyone else, as well.

"We just got back yesterday." Cameron swiped at her cheeks.

"And the first person my wife wanted to see when we got back was her old college buddy," Peter said.

"I love hearing you say, 'wife,'" Cameron teased with a wicked smile.

"Who wants a drink?" Peter said.

"I'll have the usual." Shannon loved nothing more than being with the family she chose, and these people were exactly that. There was no way in hell she would have been able to get through her childhood without them.

Annette cocked her head. On this day, they always drank beer, not her usual glass of red wine.

"Just one, though. Then Annette and I have some things to discuss."

"We don't want to home in on your alone time, but I knew you'd be here, and guess who we ran into earlier," Cameron said, elbowing Shannon in the ribs.

"Who? Was it that hot, hunky neighbor of hers? The PI guy? I've been telling her for a few months she should let him take her out on a date." Annette said, playing right into Cameron's insanity.

"I couldn't agree more," Cameron replied with the biggest smile ever.

"You all need to stop this." Shannon waved her hand in the air. "I don't need any of you meddling in my love life." She cringed. She hadn't had a *love life* in a long time, and she wouldn't have one until after she took care of something. It was time to finally make sure the past was secure where it belonged and ensure that she'd done the right thing.

"Are you saying you're dating?" Cameron planted her hands on her hips and glared. "Did something happen while I was on my honeymoon?"

"No. And I'm not going out with my neighbor." Shannon couldn't remember the last time she'd had a real date, and she didn't think being forced to walk the aisle with Peter's brother constituted a date—especially since he had a life partner.

"Well, your hot, hunky neighbor told us he's

meeting you for drinks tonight," Cameron said, smacking her lips together, making a kissing noise like a small child would. "I can't believe you didn't tell me."

"First, it's not a date. Second, he mentioned he wanted to reschedule. And third... You got home yesterday. When did you expect me to tell you about something that wasn't even a date?" Shannon's pulse doubled. Perhaps she'd be seeing Jackson tonight, after all.

But why was he acting so weirdly?

"If it wasn't a date, then what was it supposed to be?" Peter asked as he leaned against the bar.

"I wanted to hire him to help me find someone."

"Find who?" Cameron asked, her forehead wrinkled with bewilderment. One thing Cameron didn't like was not being in the know.

Shannon caught Annette's steady, all-knowing gaze.

"A client. It's a long story, and I can't really talk about it." Shannon brushed her new bangs out of her face.

"I hear Jackson and his partner are very good at finding people," Peter said, nodding his head. "You're in good hands."

"Cute hands, too." Annette winked.

Shannon glared at Annette, giving her the old evil-eye twitch.

"Oh, stop that," Annette said. "He's cute. Enjoy the eye-candy. When all is said and done, I've got money on the two of you hooking up."

"I'm in on that," Cameron said.

"Me, too," Peter piped in.

Shannon laughed. "Did you two love birds seriously come over here just to harass me about Jackson?"

"Nah. We're meeting my parents." Peter rose on tiptoe, waving. "And they're here. So, we'll catch you later."

"Are we getting together this week?" Cameron said, looping her arm through Shannon's.

"Of course, we are."

"Awesome."

Shannon watched Peter rest his hand on the small of Cameron's back as he glided her through the bar. At times, Shannon wished she'd confided in Cameron about so many things, but she just couldn't bring herself to do it. At first, she'd tried to put that part of her life in a box and stuff it into the corner. By the time she was ready to speak the truth, she felt it was too late to tell old friends.

"They're a cute couple," Annette said. "Come on, our table's ready. Let's get this show on the road. Time to celebrate our freedom."

Shannon slipped into the booth and glanced around. She'd never thought she would be at a place in her life where she could live in Lake George, much less frequent an establishment her father had often enjoyed. She scanned the restaurant for anyone who might recognize her as the young girl her father had put on display and up for sale.

Even if someone recognized her or she recognized them, no one would say a word. It wasn't the kind of thing a person acknowledged. Half the time, Shannon wanted someone to show a flicker of recognition with a huge dose of shame so she could let them know they hadn't broken her. That she'd managed to pull her life out of the hell they'd held her in and made a difference in the world.

The other half prayed no one knew who her father was.

"I do the same thing, you know?" Annette reached out, resting her warm fingers over Shannon's hand.

"Do what?"

"Please. Anytime I come to this town and see a man or woman who looks at me funny, I wonder if they know I was married to Dwight. If they were part of his circle of crazy friends and are still doing despicable things." Annette leaned across the wooden table. "I even worry that maybe someone out there—besides the two of us—suspects what I did."

"You did the one thing no one else could have or would have done for me."

"I should have done it sooner. For that, I will always be sorry."

"You have no reason to be," Shannon said. "What you did, you did out of love, and I will take that to my grave."

"I'd do it again, and I wouldn't think twice." Annette hadn't been a great stepmother, but in the end, she'd been the only adult in Shannon's life who took responsibility for what'd happened and stood by Shannon. Annette might not have been perfect, but she'd done the one thing that Shannon's own mother couldn't.

"I wish I could repay you for all you have done for me over the years," Shannon said.

"Honey, you made a life for yourself. A good one. That's payment enough."

"We need to get ourselves a couple of beers." Shannon hated beer with a passion, and not just because it had been her father's drink of choice but because she'd been forced to drink it for most of her youth. Now, once a year, she and her stepmother enjoyed her father's favorite brew and ate the meal he'd had the night he died.

The meal that'd sealed her future.

"What are we waiting for?" Shannon waved the waitress over.

"My two favorite customers." Sandy pushed out her hip, holding an order pad in her hand. Sandy was a survivor and used to be one of Shannon's patients. Shannon didn't like to socialize with any past or present clients, but Sandy had become a friend. They were about the same age, and Sandy had come to her years after her abuser died but she still hadn't been able to move her life forward.

"What can I get you two this evening?"

Shannon held up two fingers. "We'll take two orders

of the fresh bass, fried, onion rings, and bring two more beers with the meal."

"My, my. This isn't like you two. It's usually salad and wine. Is there a special occasion?"

"Once a year, we celebrate our friendship by splurging," Annette said with a big Southern smile. For years, Shannon had wanted to ask Annette if what she'd done haunted her, but then she'd have to actually acknowledge what had happened with words—and Shannon had promised Annette she never would. Besides, Annette had gone through therapy, remarried, and had a wonderful life.

Had Dwight Brendel not died, neither of them would have survived.

"I'll put the order in. If you need anything else, just let me know," Sandy said.

Shannon held up her glass in a toast. "Here's to that first day of our new lives."

They tapped their glasses together and laughed before chugging a few gulps.

The bubbles ticked Shannon's throat. The malty-yeast flavor angered her tastebuds.

Annette gagged and coughed. "Damn, that shit is fucking horrible. It's like drinking outhouse water."

"That's gross," Shannon said, shaking her head. Her stepmother had no filter, one of the things Shannon loved about her. "So, how are those grandbabies of yours?"

Annette had remarried about fifteen years ago.

George, her husband, was a kind, gentle soul, who treated her like a princess. He had three kids, two about Shannon's age, and one a few years older. All three had at least two children apiece, and Annette made for a great stepgrandmother. She thrived in her marriage, and Shannon was truly happy that Annette had been able to find real love.

The kind that lasted a lifetime.

The kind most people only dreamt about.

The kind of love Shannon prayed her little girl had because Shannon had decided to give her up.

"They are wonderful," Annette said, beaming with pride, her big, Texas smile pushing her cheeks upward. She'd aged in the last few years, with deep-set wrinkles around the eyes and lips now, but she had such a young spirit, you didn't notice the age. "You're going to be sorry you asked." Annette tapped her cell phone. "I won't go into details, but here are the latest pictures. We had a big family barbeque a couple of weeks ago." Annette lifted her gaze and scowled. "That you were invited to...but didn't come. I don't live that far away. It's only an hour and a half from here."

Shannon loved Annette for always treating her like the daughter she'd never had. Not a single family event had gone by without an issued invitation, and Shannon attended most—but never the intimate barbecues. "You know how I feel about that."

"I do. And you're wrong. George loves you, and so do all of his kids. You're always welcome in our home."

"Until my mother brings her crazy."

"Don't you dare go bringing up one incident that happened ten years ago. Besides, your mother's bark is worse than her bite, and I have no problem handling her."

"You don't have a problem handling anyone." Shannon took the phone in her hands and flipped through what seemed like a hundred images. She fought the tears threatening to fill her eyes. Annette had been her guardian angel in more ways than one. Even today, she proved to be a lifeline.

"I want you to promise me you will come to the next family gathering. I won't take no for an answer."

"It's overwhelming."

"So?" Annette took another swig of her beer. Her face scrunched, making her wrinkles double.

"I don't do the intimacy thing very well. You know that. Hell, you're the only one who knows everything. Besides my mother, who doesn't acknowledge anything, but only because that would make her look bad. Outside of my therapist, you're the only person I trust with my emotions."

Annette arched a brow. "George knows, and it's about time you start trusting some people. Sweetheart, you may not need a man, but living without intimacy… that's a lonely world. Now, promise me you will come, or I'm going to drive up and drag you kicking and screaming."

"I promise," Shannon said, knowing Annette would

never quit, and she'd also follow through on her threat. Ever since that fateful morning, Annette had gone from a young lady tossed into a world she didn't understand and trapped in an abusive marriage with no way out, to a woman who would never allow another person to take advantage of her again.

Nor would she let those she loved whimper in self-pity.

"Good. I'm going to hold you to it."

Shannon tossed her napkin over her empty plate and finished off the nasty beer by plugging her nose. "Imagine if we did this more than once a year? We'd surely die of a heart attack."

Annette smiled. "Probably, but it would be worth it."

Shannon laughed. "Agreed."

"So, I can tell something is troubling you." Annette never let her get away with anything, and she had a horrible habit of calling Shannon on her bullshit. Of all the people in her life, Annette was the only person she could count on to be brutally honest. "I'm not letting you out of here until you tell me what got under your skin."

"My mother showed up today and told me I should put a picture of my dad in my office. I know that shouldn't bother me, but it's the way she goes about shoving this crazy, screwed, false history she has of him down my throat."

Annette frowned. "Yeah. Your mom lives in fantasy land. How she can pretend it never—"

"I love you, Annette, but you don't need to say it."

"But that's part of the problem. Your mother doesn't, and you want her to at least acknowledge that it happened to you."

And that was the rub. Shannon wanted her mother to put her arms around her, hold her, and tell her that it wasn't her fault. That she hadn't done anything wrong. Just once, she wished her mother would put aside her fear of what she thought the world would see and take a closer look at her daughter and the reality she'd lived.

"We're way past that. My mother's just stressing out over my stepsister's wedding and making me unusually crazy because I have seen her more often. And you know what that does to me." Shannon knew she sounded as if she were making excuses for her mother, but she wasn't. Sadly, Shannon understood her mother more than she wanted to. "It's not about my dad, but about her having the life she thinks she deserves. And what my father did taints that. Sometimes, I think she honestly believes that no one knew my father ever cheated on her. Of course, that's why she left him."

"You're deflecting." Annette leaned back and narrowed her eyes. It was her skeptical look, and it always unnerved Shannon—more because ever since that day in her father's kitchen, Annette had developed an uncanny ability to read Shannon. She was better at it than most trained therapists.

"Stop looking at me like that." Shannon let out a

long breath before sucking in a deep one, letting her lungs fill with as much oxygen as she could.

"Your mother does this shit every year. Something else happened. I suspect it has to do with why you really hired Jackson." Annette lowered her chin. "And don't lie to me by saying you're trying to find some client."

Shannon's heart dropped to the pit of her stomach. "Do you ever wonder what became of my baby girl?"

"Yes," she said. "Every day, and you know that. But I've always respected your wishes."

"I want to know she's okay and that I did the right thing."

"You know you did the right thing, sugar," Annette said. "I'm not saying it was easy, but considering who you were back then, and your father...it was the only sane choice you could have made."

"I'm not sure I ever had a choice." Shannon felt a bubble of rage. Not that she thought she would have made a good mother, but she'd never been given a chance to choose.

Until her father died.

Annette reached across the table and grabbed Shannon's hand. "You didn't have a choice about what your father did to you. Or those men your father was involved with. But you could have made other choices when it came to the baby, and you didn't. Just like I chose to put an end to the madness."

"I thought about aborting, but it was too late."

"You were sixteen." Annette squeezed Shannon's hand hard. "You were alone. All the people who were supposed to protect you, failed you."

"You didn't."

"In a way, I did. I think, under the circumstances, you did a very brave thing by giving her up for adoption."

"Did I?" The baby girl's cry echoed in Shannon's mind. To this day, she could still conjure the sound. She'd never held her child, but she had heard her tiny voice fill her ears, and it broke her heart that she hadn't felt her daughter in her arms.

That she had no idea what her child smelled like or even looked like on the day she was born.

"Yes," Annette said with authority. "You did."

"So, you don't think I should try to find her?"

Annette pulled back and let out a big old Texas laugh. "Oh, honey," she said in her best Southern drawl. "Don't you go putting words in my mouth. But if you are asking for my opinion on the matter, if you want to know, then I say go find her. She'd be nineteen now. An adult. It would be her decision if she wanted to see and have any kind of relationship with you."

"That's what scares me. If she wanted to know me, she could have searched me out. But she hasn't."

Annette shook her head. "Don't assume anything, sugar."

"It was a closed, private adoption. If she wanted to find me, the agency would have contacted me, which hasn't happened. I don't want to insert myself into her life. I just want to know that she had a good one."

"Are you saying you don't want to meet her?"

"I don't even want to see pictures of her. I just want Jackson to find her and tell me she's okay."

Annette tilted her chin. "If you're going to take the time to find her, you should at least meet her. If she wants." She held up her hand. "I'm not going to talk you out of your plans. Only you can make this decision. Either way, I'm right behind you, but I won't ever stop speaking my mind." She leaned forward. "Isn't that why you keep me around?"

Shannon smiled. "One of the many reasons." Annette understood. *Really* understood, and that meant something. It wasn't loyalty that kept this relationship alive; it was kindness. Compassion. And unconditional love. Something that had been missing from Shannon's childhood.

And Shannon knew she needed that more than anything.

"Thank you," Shannon said, glancing at her watch. Her pulse increased at the thought of having a drink with Jackson, but at the same time, his reaction still disturbed her, and she wanted a better explanation.

She believed she deserved one.

"You and I, we've been through a lot together." Annette took her hand. "Ever since your father died, I've watched you grow into this beautiful, talented woman. You amaze me every day. But this part of your past prevents you from completely embracing your future. I want you to have everything. And I mean that."

"I know." Shannon swallowed the emotional sob that threatened to escape.

"Go home and talk with Jackson. Do this one final thing so you can have all the happiness you deserve."

Shannon knew Annette was right. Finding her daughter was the final link to her healing.

CHAPTER THREE

Shannon sank into the plastic chair in front of the fire pit between her place and Jackson's, where she could see the road and the lake—though she could do without that damned sailboat taunting her, reminding her of one of the biggest reasons why she'd opted not to keep her baby girl.

The moon and the stars danced in the near-black sky, casting wonderful streaks of light in the matching dark lake below. The sail lines of the Tartan rattled against the tall mast. So many memories flooded her as the sound pricked her ears. Sailing hadn't always been a horrible experience. At times, she'd be out there, feeling the cool wind on her face as the bow cut through the three-foot whitecaps, that it had been as exhilarating as free falling during a bungee jump at the local amusement park.

Until her father and his crew forever changed her perception of sailing.

She took in a deep breath and focused on the present and her future.

Annette was right. She'd done everything in her power over the last nineteen years to make a better life and put the pains of her childhood behind her—except for one thing. And it was time to put all the pieces of the puzzle together and mend her broken heart.

An engine's growl grew closer. She fought the desire not to look over her shoulder, but her heart won out.

Not Jackson this time.

She had to make Jackson understand and take her case. She couldn't trust this to a complete stranger. It was the one thing from her past that still sat in the pit of her stomach like a boulder that couldn't be moved.

The roar of a diesel followed by headlights beaming through the trees sent her pulse racing. With a shaky hand, she lifted her glass of wine and gulped. Not once, but twice. She needed every ounce of courage she could muster.

He parked his truck next to her two-door coupe. "Hey," he said as he sauntered up the walkway between the two cottages. "Sorry I'm late."

"You've been sending me mixed messages, so I wasn't sure if you were going to show or not." She pointed to a glass on the small plastic end table that matched her plastic Adirondack chair. "Help yourself. It's a really nice Merlot."

"Don't mind if I do, but I'm afraid I'll break your plastic chairs," he said as he effortlessly lifted one off the ground. "You really need to get rid of these things and get some real wooden ones like I have." He pointed across the shared patio as he lowered himself, adjusting the chair in the grass as if it were about to crack and break at any second. Stretching out his long legs, he showed off his tan Timberland boots and his worn jeans. A button-down flannel hid his toned torso that she looked forward to seeing as summer took over spring.

"Yeah, I know. I keep saying I will, but I never get around to it."

He looked out toward the lake, raised the glass to his lips, then lowered it just a tad and said, "I owe you an apology."

"Why is that?" Shannon studied his strong profile. She had to agree but wanted to hear his reasons.

His facial expressions didn't change much, which she suspected he was well aware of and had done on purpose. Before he'd become a PI, he'd been a police officer, though he rarely talked about it. All she knew was that he'd been mortally wounded, somehow recovered, received a medal, and retired.

"For the way I behaved this morning." He turned. The light from the fire reflected in his dark eyes. "I want to talk with you about why I said no. But first, I want to give you a report on your friend."

"All right." She shifted in her chair, trying not to appear too nervous. But given how he gave her a reassuring smile, she knew she hadn't been successful.

"Miss Montgomery's boss said she took a few days off work."

"How did you know where she worked? I didn't tell you that." Shannon bit down on her tongue. "I'm sorry. I'm sure you have your ways."

He chuckled. "I generally don't tell people about cases I'm working on, but someone had already hired me to find Belinda."

"Find? By whom?" Her voice screeched, cutting through the night like a hissing raccoon.

"My business, in a way, is similar to yours. Client confidentiality. But I'm going to break it because I think we need to work together on this one." He shifted, taking off his cowboy hat and setting it on the chair next to him.

"What exactly does that mean?" She fiddled with her necklace, her heart fluttering like a hummingbird hovering over a bird feeder.

"I'm at a loss with this one, and I need you to help me find her." He ran a hand through his hair. "As a private investigator, I would have come knocking on your door tomorrow morning anyway."

Shannon swallowed. "I can't tell you anything," she said. "I shouldn't have even asked you to look for her."

"We can pretend that you didn't. Now, please. Find a way to give me something. She didn't go home last Thursday, and the last people to see her were a few tellers at her place of business. We are at a dead end. Her roommate is filing a missing person's report, so we hope we get something on that, but I'm not putting my money on it."

"That's not good." Shannon chugged the rest of her wine before pouring another glass. "I'm going to assume that my name will get brought into this somehow, and I'll be getting a visit from the police." She folded her feet under her butt and then turned her head to catch his stare. "You mentioned that her employer said she had taken some time off. So, why the missing person's report?"

"Because what I've found out doesn't add up. Her boss said she went on a trip with her boyfriend. Her roommate said she and her boyfriend broke up."

"I see," Shannon said.

He tipped his glass. "That's all you have to say on the subject? What about her roommate? Did they get along?"

Shannon shook her head. "We need to stop this line of discussion. I won't break doctor-patient confidentiality unless I'm handed a subpoena, and that isn't going to happen on a missing person's case unless foul play is suspected."

"That's true. But I'll be honest, I've got a bad feeling

about this one." He held her gaze for a long moment and then leaned back in his chair.

"If you have information that clearly shows she's in danger, I might be able to help more, but if you can't, then we're stuck in a situation where I can't comment on certain things."

"Will you let me know if the police come knocking on your door?" Jackson closed his eyes, remaining still.

"I will call you if that happens." She continued studying him, but he didn't give up any of his tells. Nope. He remained still. Quiet. He barely moved, other than to drink his wine, and even then, he gave nothing away.

He laughed. "You might consider being a little more subtle when you're sizing someone up."

"When people walk into my office, they expect me to shrink them. They try to deflect and use body language they learned on television or in a book. It never works."

"We're not in your office." He shifted in his chair and looked her in the eye. "And you do this every time we talk."

"Hazard of the job." She shrugged.

"And what have you concluded?"

"You're an enigma."

His laugh cut through the thick air. "Perhaps I am. But I also frighten you," he said.

"What makes you say that?" She pinched the silver pendant between her fingers. He'd nailed that one, but she wondered if he knew *why* he utterly terrified her.

"You're playing with your necklace. You do that when you're uncomfortable, and you seem to always do that around me."

She dropped her hand into her lap. "It's not you I'm afraid of. But I will admit, I was scared to tell you about my daughter. Only a couple of people know. It's not something I talk about."

"I understand. And again, I'm sorry about the way I reacted."

She squirmed, sitting on her hand to keep from fiddling with her necklace. "Sorry enough that you'll take my case?"

"I have a personal reason for not wanting to take it," he said. His right eye twitched, and for the first time since she'd known him, his voice rose an octave.

"What's that?"

"I was adopted," he said, reaching out his hand and placing it on her arm. "Meeting my birth mother ended badly."

"I had no idea you were adopted." She shrugged his hand away, feeling patronized.

He cocked his head. "Do you want to hear why I don't want to take your case?"

Shannon nodded.

"Her motives weren't in my best interests and only served herself. She didn't care about me or my feelings. And she didn't care about my parents or my sisters. It affected my entire family. That's why I generally recommend a friend in these types of cases."

"I don't want to work with a friend of yours. I want *you* to take the case." She bit down on her tongue. "And I'm not your mother."

"I'll consider it, depending on why you want to find to find her."

"So, if my answer meets your requirement, then you'll do it. Otherwise, I get pawned off?" Fuck it. She reached for her pendant, fingering it once again. It didn't lower her heart rate, but it did stop her from wanting to tell Jackson she'd made a mistake and march into her house.

"You can look at it that way if you want. But the truth is, I want to help you. I just need to know why it's so important to you."

As long as she didn't get into the details of what'd happened, that should be an easy enough question to answer. Only her mind searched for the words, and none formed.

She cleared her throat. "I was sixteen and scared shitless. In a bad situation all around."

"I'm sorry that you had to go through that. And I don't mean to belittle your situation, but lots of young girls find themselves pregnant and unsure of what to do. Sadly, it's not uncommon."

There was nothing typical about what had happened to her, but she wouldn't go down that path. Not today.

Not ever.

Not with Jackson.

"And that doesn't tell me anything about why you want to find her."

"I just want to know she had a good life. That by me giving her up, I gave her a better life. Once I know that, I will step away and continue to let her live it. Hell, I don't even want to meet her. I just need to know."

Jackson tossed back the rest of his wine before folding his arms across his chest. "How is knowing who she is going to make you take a step back and leave her alone?"

"Wow. That's really unfair. I've spent almost nineteen years knowing that I couldn't be a good mother, and all I want—"

"You think you can be a mother now?" he asked behind a tight jaw as he jumped from the plastic chair, sending it tumbling into the grass. "I don't understand women like you. You give up a child. Just walk away. And that's fine. I get it, and God, I value that decision. It was the best thing my birth mother ever did for me. But then you think it's perfectly okay to go poking around in that child's life, expecting them to be all warm, welcoming, and grateful to see you without thinking about what that might do to the child or the families they grew up in?"

If she were in the confines of her office, she wouldn't be shocked by the venom-laced words, and she'd be able to process his emotions from the caring yet objective perspective of a therapist.

But she'd put her heart on the line, and he'd squeezed the blood out of it like he knew what her life had been like.

"If I wanted to be beaten up emotionally for giving up a child, I would be having this conversation with my own mother. I don't want to find her to make a mommy connection or anything. And, frankly, I resent you making rash judgments about me." She took in a deep breath through her nose and let it out through her mouth, counting to four. "What happened between you and your birth mother that left you so angry and resentful?"

"It doesn't matter."

"Like hell, it doesn't. You're drawing conclusions about me, my decisions, and what I want before ever letting me tell you my reason why—all based on your own personal experience."

"You just told me your reasons."

"Not really." This was getting deeper than she wanted.

"All right." He smoothed his hair before picking up the chair. "Why don't you tell me why you need to find her?"

"Okay. But not until you take a seat."

He nodded.

"And I want you to tell me what happened with your birth mother."

He arched a brow.

"You're refusing services because of what happened to you. If I'm going to plead my case, and you still refuse, I feel you at least owe me the rationale behind it."

"Fair enough."

She poured another hefty glass of wine. "All I want is to know that I did the right thing. That she has a better life than I could have ever given her," she said.

"And what if she didn't have a good life?" he asked. "Have you thought about that?"

Shannon sucked in a quick breath. "Yes. As a matter of fact, I have. And if something bad happened, I will have to live with that."

"Can you?"

"Jesus. Just give me the name of your friend. I'll have them find her."

He reached out and encircled his fingers around her wrist. "You gave her up for a reason. You own that reason. But once you made that decision, you gave up getting to own the outcome."

"I understand that." She slid her arm out from under his grip. "But I need to know."

"Do you? Or do you, deep down, want to meet your daughter?"

"You have no idea what it's like not knowing anything about a person you gave birth to. I need to know she exists. That those cries I heard when she was born were real."

Jackson had moved his chair so it faced hers, and it made it very difficult not to look at him. "What does that mean?"

She blinked. "I don't know how to make it any clearer. I need to know what happened to her."

"I know I sound like a broken record, but what if what I find out isn't good?"

Tears formed in her eyes. "Anything is better than not knowing she exists. Will you help me or not?"

"You don't want any contact with her?"

Shannon shook her head. "I understand how disruptive that could be, even if my intentions are good. That's why I don't want to meet her. But to know she's out there... Somewhere. It would ease my aching heart."

He touched the side of her cheek. Gently, he took his forefinger and brushed part of her hair behind her ear. "I know what it's like to want to know of someone's existence. It's natural and normal. But the outcome isn't always what we expect."

"I can't let it go," she admitted.

"I'll find her," he whispered, tracing her jawline. His chocolate orbs were as dark as the evening sky, and they seemed to reach into her soul. They were kind and gentle eyes. Caring. The palm of his hand cupped her cheek, and he drew her face toward him. He kissed her forehead and then wrapped both of his hands around her and held her close.

Every muscle in her body loosened, and she leaned

in to this strong man and cried. Really cried. "I'm sorry. I don't mean to be so emotional."

"Yeah, you do," he said, still running one hand up and down her back while the other cradled her head. "My sisters and I have always known we were adopted, but each of us always wondered at some point in our life why we had been given away. I'd be lying if I didn't feel tossed aside and unloved by my birth parents. My adoptive mom, my *real* mother, told me that having a child was a selfish act. That she wanted a child so badly, she would have done anything. But that giving one away had to be the most selfless act, and she couldn't imagine what that must have been like for my birth mother to trust her son to another family."

Shannon wiped her tears from her cheeks and pushed away from his comforting embrace. "Did you seek out your birth mother?"

He shook his head. "She sought me out. She was a con artist and never really wanted to get to know me, but I learned that the hard way."

"Were you mad at your adoptive mom for filling your head with ideas that she had no idea were true or not?"

He laughed. "You really need to learn to be more subtle when going into doctor-mode."

"Sorry. I have a horrible habit of doing that when someone gives me that much information about a painful experience. But it's also a deflection, and it's helping me suck up the tears. I really hate crying."

"Cry all you want. Doesn't bother me. Remember, I have five sisters. But feel free to deflect all you want, too. My oldest sister is a master at that." He winked. "And to answer your question, yes. I felt like my parents lied to me, but how were they to know my birth mother was a lunatic? In a weird way, I owe her a huge thank you for doing the right thing and giving me up."

"Can I ask you a personal question?"

"That's funny, considering one of my hands is on your thigh, and the other is massaging your shoulder."

"Now who's deflecting?" She should push him away. Having any kind of intimate contact with him wouldn't end well. "Would you have looked for your birth parents if she hadn't come looking for you?"

"I don't know," he said. "Two of my sisters went looking for theirs, and it turned out okay, but that just brings me back to the idea that it should be up to the person who was given up, not the birth parents."

"I do understand your reasoning regarding that."

"And I understand yours. Which is why I'm willing to take the case."

"Thank you." She pulled back, needing to break the physical contact. "Everything I know is in a small envelope inside. It was a closed adoption." She stood. "I'll go get it."

"Take your time."

She entered the house. The envelope sat in the drawer of a small table in the hallway by the stairs. She picked it up and held it close to her chest. It was thin. And light. A few pieces of paper. That was it.

Shannon took a deep breath, then went back onto the porch. Jackson had stretched his legs out again, ankles crossed. One hand rested behind his head, the other held the glass of wine.

She placed the envelope in his lap. "Thank you," she said.

"You're welcome." He pointed to the chair. "Now, sit, and let's enjoy the view."

"I really don't want to talk anymore."

He reached out and took her hand. "Neither do I. But I don't want the evening to end."

Reluctantly, she joined him, still holding his hand. He didn't let go. And he didn't talk.

It was the nicest thing any man had done for her in years.

———

"Oh, shit," Shannon's sweet voice startled Jackson.

He turned to face her. "What's the matter?"

Shannon bolted upright, yanking her hand from his, snapping him from the visions of kissing her goodnight.

If he got the nerve.

He'd always had a bit of an ego when it came to women, and no one would ever call him shy.

Reserved? Absolutely.

Shy? When hell froze over.

But this woman had made his heart race like a lovesick schoolboy with a crush on a teacher. About the only thing he could do was hold her hand and fantasize like a stupid boy. Otherwise, he might make an ass out of himself, and that just wasn't an option.

"I need to do something." She leaned over, kicking off her shoes and rolling up her pant legs.

"What are you doing?"

"I need to go dip my toes in the water before midnight."

He reached over and picked up her shoe. "So, am I Prince Charming or the driver of the pumpkin coach?"

She paused, staring at him with a scrunched face. "Would you mind coming down to the dock with me?"

"Not at all. But I'm not getting in the water. Last I checked, it was still cold as ice." He stood, taking her by the hand, and led her down the long, windy path. "Can I ask why we are doing this?"

"It's just something I do on the anniversary of my father's death."

"Maybe you want to be alone?" There was no love lost between him and his birth mother, and he didn't want to think about the day when his real parents died.

So far, they were both healthy as horses, but that didn't change the fact that they weren't getting any younger.

Nor had they let up on their desire to have the

family name carried on. All of his sisters had children, but none with their last name: Armstrong.

At thirty-nine, Jackson still didn't feel the need to have a child, something the woman standing next to him would probably have a field day with during a therapy session.

"Normally, I'd say yes. But I usually do it in the morning, and your boat threw me for a loop."

"Are you afraid of the water or something?"

"No. Just sailboats."

"I know a really great therapist that could help you with that." He hoped his attempt at humor didn't get him pushed into the freezing water. He wasn't sure if he should ask her what the toe-dipping meant. She hadn't offered much information, but something told him this wasn't going to be a typical ode to the old man. Jackson got the impression that Shannon's relationship with her father had been complicated.

Whatever the reason for the ritual and her fear of boats, he could hold her hand and be there for her.

It was the neighborly thing to do.

He nearly laughed out loud. While he wanted to support Shannon, he also wanted to kiss her. Maybe even more.

He paused at the edge of the dock, staring down at his sneakers. "Do you want me to join you?"

"If you want. But I'll warn you, it's a strange ritual. You won't understand, and I'm not going to explain it." Her curtness caught him off guard. He wanted to ask a few more questions, but the closer they got to the edge of the dock, the more her body tensed. He could feel the wrath seeping from her skin like fog rising from the lake.

Shedding his boots and socks, he sat on the edge of the dock.

The ice-cold water gripped his feet. He shuddered.

Shannon dangled hers over the dock, the water lapping at her ankles. She leaned over and spit.

What the fuck?

"The only good thing you ever did for me was die. I hope you're rotting in hell," she whispered.

Well, that was certainly unexpected. "You can't expect me not to ask questions after that."

"My father wasn't a very nice man." She jumped to her feet, and the dock rattled as she stomped toward the path.

"Wait a second." He stood, nearly toppling into the water. "Don't run off, Shannon."

"I'm not. It's late, my feet are cold, and I want to go to bed." She quickened her pace to a jog, not looking over her shoulder.

"Stop," he called, but she just kept going.

He took off running, making it to her patio only two paces behind her. "I'm worried about you."

"I'm fine. Really." She snagged her heels. "I'm sorry. I shouldn't have asked you to come with me. I know your boat can't hurt me, but it's so much like the one my father owned, and it just stirred up a lot of bad shit on a day that, for me, is a celebration."

"A celebration? What the hell did your father do to you?" He clenched his hands into fists. He didn't need her to answer. The combination of sadness, fear, and fury coming from her normally sweet blue eyes said it all.

"It doesn't matter."

"To toss your words back at you, *like hell it doesn't*, or you wouldn't bother with the ritual." He'd seen his fair share of battered women and children as a cop. The survivors always carried the same resolve to prove they were fine. But no matter how long ago the abuse happened, a bit of that fear always clung to them like a wound that never quite healed. "I'm sorry your father hurt you."

She reached up, palming his cheek with her soft hand. "It was a long time ago, and I do this every year to remind myself that I didn't deserve it and that I'm making a difference in this world despite having had a difficult childhood. I know it seems strange, and I probably looked like some crazy, angry—"

He pressed his finger to her plump lips. "You're far from crazy."

"Thanks, Jackson. You're a good man." She dropped her hand, taking a step back.

"I could probably park the boat down the street at the marina if it makes you that uncomfortable."

She shook her head. "That's just silly. It's fine, really.

Thanks for helping me tonight. Oh, I completely forgot to ask…" Her eyes went wide.

"Ask what?" He wondered if she needed to do some other ritualistic thing. He wasn't so sure he wanted to be a part of it.

But he would if she asked.

"How much do you charge? I'm sure you'll need some kind of retainer."

"A hundred dollars should be enough for me to get the un-identifying information about the adoption. After that, I'll give you the friends and family discount of fifty dollars an hour."

"I don't want to take advantage of you."

The corners of his mouth tugged upward. "This is probably going to be the most inappropriate thing I could say, but I wouldn't mind you taking advantage of me at all."

"Good night, Jackson." She pushed open her door. "Maybe we can have dinner this weekend."

"Are you asking me on a date?"

"Maybe." And with that, Shannon disappeared into her house.

He'd lost his ever-loving mind. He had rules for a reason, and he never broke them.

Only, he'd broken two tonight.

Never take on an adoption case with a birth parent.

And never, ever go out with a client.

CHAPTER FOUR

Jackson pulled out a new file, put Shannon's name on it with a green Sharpie, and opened the contents of the envelope she had given him the night before. He thumbed through the records, which wasn't much. The name of the hospital. Date and time of birth. The fact that the baby had been a girl. Shannon's name but no birth father.

He took a pad and pencil and started making some notes when his partner Katie strolled into the office.

She carried herself with an air of confidence. One that he knew she drew from lies, betrayal, and loneliness. She had a good heart, though it had hardened the moment her uncle went to prison for trying to kill her. "God, I hate the smell of paint. Will the odor ever go away?" she asked as she took off her baseball cap and hung it on the coat rack next to the door.

"Good morning to you, too," he said with a big smile.

"Westerfield asked me to give this to you." She dumped a sealed envelope onto his desk before she clicked across the office in her high heels. She lifted a bouquet of red and yellow tulips he'd brought in this morning. "Why do you do things like this?"

Her desk sat directly across from his in their large office space. Originally, it had been two offices, but neither of them liked having to go back and forth to talk to each other, so they knocked down the wall. They also had a small reception area. One day, they hoped to make enough money to hire a receptionist to put behind the humble empty desk. On the other side of the reception area lay a small conference room.

The building itself stood four stories, and they occupied the second floor. The first level held an insurance company, and Bryant and Bangle, Attorneys at Law—their biggest clients and landlords—occupied the top two floors.

"You have to admit, they brighten up the place, along with the freshly painted walls," he said.

"Yeah. Yeah. Your mother should have named you Jessica, not Jackson." She sat behind her desk and fired up her computer. "Any messages?"

"Not a single one," he said.

"So, what's on the agenda for today?" she asked, her fingers pounding on the keyboard, her stare engaged only with the screen. Most people looked at Katie and saw a rebel without a cause. An angry woman with an ax to grind.

Behind her tough exterior and fiery red hair hid a scared little girl who wanted answers to questions only her incarcerated uncle or dead mother could give her.

"We've got two appointments with potential new clients. One is a let's-spy-on-my-wife case, and the other is with an insurance company looking to hire us to do investigative work on some worker's comp cases."

"Hate insurance companies," she said. "Wouldn't the flowers look better on the conference table today?"

He laughed. "Already put some there."

"Of course, you did," she said. "You're a great work wife."

"I'm here to make you happy." He opened the envelope from Westerfield, his buddy over at the Warren County sheriff's office. "Well, shit." He stared at the name printed on the report for the owner of the blue sedan that had been parked at the top of his and Shannon's drive.

Ned Brendel.

"What's the problem?"

"I don't know yet." Just because the car's registered owner had the same last name as Shannon, didn't mean they were related. "Hey, Siri, call Westerfield."

His buddy answered on the second ring. "What's up, man?"

"Thanks for the printout. Do you know anything about this guy?"

"You obviously didn't read my sticky note on the third page. He's your neighbor's uncle."

"You don't say. Anything else?" Jackson asked.

"I ran a check. Found a sealed juvenile report on Ned Brendel. I'm trying to get my hands on it. I'll send it over when and if I get it."

"Thanks." Jackson tapped the red button on the cell. He set the phone on the desk, screen up, twirling it with his index finger.

"What has you so deep in thought?" Katie plopped her ass down on the side of his desk.

He pushed Shannon's file across the wood.

"I can't believe you took on an adoption case. You've given me shit every single time, and now *you're* going to do it because you've got the hots for your neighbor."

"I'm not doing it because I find Shannon attractive."

"I can't think of any other reason for you to do it. Because you damn near quit on me the last time." Katie held up the birth certificate. "Wow. Sixteen. I tell you, Dr. Shannon Brendel doesn't seem the type to have sex as a teenager."

"Shut up," Jackson said. "We were all young and stupid once."

"You know that's not how I meant it. It's just that she seems so put-together. It surprises me she'd be in a situation where she'd have to give up a baby when she was just a kid herself."

"If that's the case, then stop getting bent out of shape whenever someone makes a judgment about you because of your uncle."

Katie knocked on the desk with a knuckle. "That's hitting below the belt."

The sound of footsteps coming from the stairs caught Jackson's attention.

He checked his watch. "Saved by our client, who is early." Jackson would have loved to go a round or two with Katie. One of these days, he hoped to get her to understand that she wasn't an extension of her family —or their dysfunction.

A young man stepped across the threshold.

"May I help you?" Jackson asked.

"I think someone from this office called me."

"Who are you?" Jackson hadn't met their scheduled first appointment of the day, but he knew without a doubt that this wasn't him.

"Ben Nisson. I used to date Belinda Montgomery."

Well, shit. Maybe they were about to get their first break.

"Come on in," Katie said, waving the young man in.

Jackson closed the door and pointed to the seat next to Katie's desk. "Have a seat."

The young man wore tan slacks and a crisply pressed blue button-down shirt that reminded Jackson of the nerds that worked for the Geek Squad.

"I came right over as soon as I got the message," Ben said.

"Why didn't you just call us back?" Katie asked. "We're a long way from Saratoga."

"Actually, only twenty minutes." Ben's foot rattled the floorboards. "But my cousin lives up here, and I was visiting with him."

"For how long?" Jackson scribbled his observations about Ben on the notepad.

Nervous.

Avoids eye contact.

Terrified. But of what?

"Just for a long weekend. Fishing trip."

Jackson nodded. "I love fishing."

Katie cocked her head, knowing he hated tossing a line over.

"Tell us, Ben, when was the last time you saw your girlfriend?" Jackson went for the bang.

"I don't have a girlfriend." Ben turned and gazed out the window. "Not anymore, anyway."

"When did that happen?" Katie leaned back in her chair.

Jackson cringed, waiting for her to toss her feet up onto the desk and start twirling her gum.

If she had gum.

"We broke up about a month ago," Ben said. "I haven't talked to or seen her in weeks. She won't take my calls anymore. Did something happen to her? Is that why you called me?"

"We don't know if anything happened," Katie said, leaning forward and folding her arms on her desk. "Do you?"

He shook his head. His eyes teared.

Katie never believed anyone who cried.

Jackson only believed the ones who tried to act as though crying were the tell all by itself. This kid didn't even try to hide his tears, but he sure as hell didn't bring attention to them.

"Why did you break up?" Jackson asked.

Ben snapped his gaze to Jackson. "She started dating someone else. I don't know who, but she made it clear that she was done with me." He looked from Katie to Jackson then back to Katie. "Did something happen to her?" he asked again. "Please, tell me."

"We really don't know anything," Jackson repeated. "All we know is that she took some time off work. Any idea where she might have gone?"

"She's always wanted to go to the Sagamore Hotel. Spend a few days there. She talked about it all the time, but I couldn't afford to take her."

"Anywhere else?" Katie asked.

Ben rubbed his red cheek with a shaky hand. "If anything happened to her, I'll never forgive myself. I got so mad at her when she dumped me that I told her I hoped she rotted in hell."

"I think we've all done things in the heat of the moment we regret," Katie said with a soft, soothing tone. It didn't happen often, but when she tried, she could really be a caring woman.

"Can I asked who hired you?" Ben asked.

Katie and Jackson glanced at each other.

Jackson nodded. Normally, he wouldn't divulge this kind of information, but under the cirucumstances, he wanted to gauge Ben's reaction.

"Her roommate, Janice," Katie said.

"Seriously? They hate each other." Ben shook his head. "I mean, knock-down-and-drag-out fight kind of hate. Belinda had talked about moving out." Ben's bright eyes dulled. "I told her she could move in with me, but that didn't happen."

"Janice paints a different picture of her relationship with Belinda," Jackson said.

"That's shocking. But I don't really know Janice well. We never spent much time at Belinda's place, always crashing at mine."

"Until a month ago," Katie added just to scare the crap out of the young man, hoping he'd spill the beans.

If he had beans to spill.

"Will you let me know when you find her?" Ben stood, shoving his hands into his pockets. "I just want to know she's okay."

"Sure. But please let us know if you hear from her or think of anything that might help us." Jackson stood, escorting the young man to the door. "We'll be in touch."

"This case is getting interesting," Katie said.

Jackson had to agree, only he didn't necessarily like interesting.

"I think it's time for you to call your new girlfriend and put the pressure on."

"She's not my girlfriend, and I already did. She won't give us much unless we have a subpoena or Belinda is in danger."

"Try again. Because if we wait for the cops, it's going to be too late."

Jackson had to agree.

———

Shannon's purse vibrated. She dug into the bag, hoping she found it before the light turned red. Walking across the street while doing anything but putting one foot in front of the other could prove to be a dangerous action.

Jackson's number flashed across her screen. "Hey. What's up?" Her heart hammered against her rib cage. Besides wanting to know if he had any news on her daughter, just hearing his voice gave her the kind of decadent pleasure that licking the brownie batter off the spatula had given her as a child.

Sweet.

Devilish.

And wrong.

But oh, so good.

"I got a visit from Ben Nisson this morning."

"Oh, really?" Well, talking about work squashed her

mood right quick, especially when she wasn't supposed to be talking about Belinda's private sessions with Jackson.

"So, you know him?"

"No. Never met the fellow," she said, tapping her foot, waiting for the pedestrian signal. "But I might have heard of him. From, you know, a mutual friend."

"We going to talk in code now. Cool." Jackson chuckled. "Did you know Belinda dumped him a couple of weeks ago?"

"That's a rumor I didn't hear." Shannon had spent hours listening to Belinda go on and on about how much she loved Ben but how he didn't understand her or her issues. Of course, Shannon didn't think Belinda had been completely upfront with her boyfriend about having been a sex worker, but who could blame her?

"Really?" Jackson asked.

"But I heard that a man had shown her a lot of interest in front of Ben. No idea who. She never mentioned a name or where she knew him from. Only that someone other than Ben had been giving her a lot of attention. I think she wanted to use the new guy to make Ben jealous."

"Interesting on two accounts."

"What does that mean?" Shannon looked both ways before stepping into the intersection. Walking and talking wasn't a talent she'd mastered.

"Ben flat-out said she dumped him for a new guy, and you're giving me a lot of information regarding a patient that you said you wouldn't. I thought I would have to sweet talk you to get it."

"Actually, I gathered that piece of information when I ran into Belinda at the bank while making a deposit. She'd been on a break and asked to chat. That was two days before she missed our *lunch,* and not during a session."

"I see," Jackson said. "I've got something else I need to discuss with you."

"I have to meet with a patient at the hospital in a few minutes. It might run through dinner, but want to meet at the fire pit in a couple of hours?"

Say, yes. Please, just say yes.

"Sounds like a plan. See you then."

"Looking forward to it." She ended the call.

Shannon crossed the road with a new spring in her step.

She'd deal with her patient, then go home, pour a glass of wine, and enjoy an evening with Jackson. She'd tortured herself enough over the years. At thirty-six, she had the world in the palm of her hand. She'd beaten the odds. And now, maybe, just maybe, she'd be able to really let go and let a man in.

Even if for only a short time.

Shannon entered the hospital through the main emergency doors. Though she had many patients come through the ER, she wasn't a regular, but everyone knew who she was. She took a slight detour down the side corridor to snag a cup of coffee and two candy bars—plain chocolate for her, and a Snickers for Gretchen.

She took the long way to the psych ward, giving her a few moments to collect her thoughts. She smiled as the evening security guard noticed her coming down the hall.

"Good evening," Kent said.

Kent couldn't have been more than twenty-two, but he'd been working this post for the last three years. He always greeted her with a smile, and tonight was no different. "Haven't seen you here in a while."

"That's a good thing," she said, patting him on the shoulder then handing him the cup of coffee.

"You're the best. No one else brings shitty-ass hospital coffee." He buzzed her through the doors.

The moment they swung open, her muscles tightened with anxiety, and depression swallowed her heart. She forced a smile as she signed the appropriate paperwork and then asked for the nurse on duty to page the doctor on call.

Dr. Franklin was her least favorite psychiatrist in the hospital because he viewed psychologists as beneath him. He never came out and said that anyone who hadn't gone to medical school wasn't capable of treating the mentally ill, but he was always condescending in his tone.

And he had a constant need to be right.

What sucked was that nine out of ten times, he was.

"Shannon," Dr. Franklin said as he strolled leisurely

up to the nurses' station, refusing the professional courtesy of using her doctor title. "We're still waiting on the toxicology report, but according to the patient, she ingested a half a bottle of antidepressants after freebasing cocaine, drinking at least a pint of vodka, and she thinks she might have taken some ecstasy, as well," he said without a trace of emotion. "After her body detoxes, I've prescribed a combination of medications to deal with the bi-polar issues. It is imperative that she stay on the medications."

Shannon opened her mouth to say, "Thank you," but before she could get the words out, Franklin hushed her with his hand.

"I know you prefer non-medication treatment," he said. "But in this case, it is necessary. Please, trust me on this. She has a better chance of staying away from the other chemicals if her mood is more efficiently balanced, and I also recommended she seek out a different type of therapy after she is released."

"That will be up to *my* patient." Shannon dug her nails into the side of her thigh. The fact that *her* patient had landed herself in the psych ward didn't give Shannon any reason to pat herself on the back for being an excellent therapist. If anything, it proved the exact opposite. But she didn't need this asshole jumping down her throat because he had a problem with PhDs over medical school degrees.

Or maybe it was women over men.

"As far as the medication goes, I have worked

closely with her primary care physician for the right meds. If she takes them like she's supposed to, her mood stabilizes." Shannon knew she shouldn't pick a fight with this guy, but it was too late to take it back. "It took a while for us to find the right combination with the right dosage. I will make sure her primary gets you the exact combination and dosage tonight."

"I've already requested them. However, it's obvious that this course of treatment isn't working. This is her third time in the unit."

"Not for an attempted suicide." She raised her hand to keep the pain-in-the-ass doctor from speaking. "And just so we are straight, you are the one who made that judgment call when she arrived. So, this is visit number one under those circumstances."

"That's not the point," Dr. Franklin said. "I will be recommending a different course of treatment."

"Recommend all you want," she said under her breath. "But I'm her therapist, and even though you are the doctor on call, she's still *my* patient. So, back off and let me do my job."

Dr. Franklin blinked but otherwise remained still. "We'll hold her for forty-eight hours, and then we can discuss what will be the most appropriate medication and psychotherapy." With a wave of his hand, Dr. Franklin dismissed Shannon. "Miss Carson is in room four." He nodded over his shoulder before stepping around Shannon.

"I can't believe you stood up to him," the nurse said.

She must have been new because Shannon had never seen her before. "No way could I ever talk to a doctor like that," the nurse continued.

"Doctors aren't God." Shannon took a mental note of the young girl's name spelled out on a tag across her colorful scrubs. "Erica, are you Gretchen's nurse?"

She nodded. "I'll be here until midnight."

"Great." She pulled out her card. "Call me if Dr. Franklin continues acting like an ass when it comes to my patient, okay?"

"I can't go against him. Or any doctor."

"All I'm asking is to be informed if Franklin goes against my recommendations. Can you do that?"

"Yeah. I can manage that," Erica said.

"Thanks." All Shannon wanted to do at this point was assess her patient and go home.

To be with Jackson.

This part of the psych ward was referred to as the *holding tank*. It consisted of one small nurses' station and one large room partitioned off by six curtains creating six patient *rooms*. The curtain to room four was completely drawn.

Shannon took a deep breath and let it out slowly as she pulled the ugly green shade. She smiled at Gretchen.

"Hey," Gretchen managed. "Fancy meeting you here." More anger than humor laced her sarcasm, but her eyes showed a sadness in her soul. "Shocked it's not my funeral?"

"Thought you might like this." Shannon placed the Snickers bar on the side of the bed, ignoring the bait to engage Gretchen in a battle of you-really-don't-care-so-why-are-you-bothering banter.

"That other doctor gave me a whole bunch." Gretchen pointed to the rolling table. "A lot more than you brought.

"That was kind of him," Shannon said.

"It sure was. God knows I need some sugar, and this place sucks ass. I bet if I had a real doctor and not some stupid therapist, I'd be out of this joint."

Gretchen was good at the blame game. Normally, she'd toss it all at her mother. She had enough ammunition with her lack of parental support, along with a history of abuse that, to her, it was no surprise she'd turned out the way she had. To be able to turn her life around, Gretchen needed to understand how her internal monologue related to the triggers in her addiction. That meant self-awareness. Currently, she had very little.

Shannon pulled up a chair and sat down. "How are you feeling?"

"How do you think I feel?" Gretchen turned her head and grinned. "I'm just peachy." She reached for the Snickers and ripped it open. "I want the fuck out of this place. Can you make that happen?"

Shannon shook her head.

"I bet Dr. Franklin could. He's a real doctor. I'm in here because of you."

"You took a lethal dose of pills and recreational drugs. On purpose. When you got here, you were barely breathing." If Gretchen were to get better, she had to own up to her actions.

That said, given her agitation, the way her fingers twitched, and how her hands shook, she was still high, coming down from all the drugs and going into withdrawal.

"Spare me the lecture," Gretchen said. "I got things mixed up and thought I was taking something else. Besides, if you'd had my day, you'd want to take a bunch of mind-numbing, completely legal drugs, too."

"Not an entire bottle. And not all the drugs you took were legal." Shannon picked up the chart and scanned the documents. "So, what happened to trigger such anger and the need to escape?"

"Like telling you the events of the day is going to change anything," Gretchen said with a mouth full of nuts and chocolate. "But if you must know, I went to my mother's."

"Really?" Shannon didn't like that she sounded so shocked, but the reality was that Gretchen's mother didn't care about her children and was toxic when it came to Gretchen. "When?"

Gretchen brushed back her unruly auburn hair, showing a nasty bruise on her face. "I showed up unannounced for lunch."

"You have a restraining order out on your mother,

you shouldn't have done that. Did she put that bruise on your face?"

"Yeah." Gretchen nodded. "I guess I puked all over her new white carpet, and she thought hitting me fit the crime."

"So, you went to your mother's wasted?"

Gretchen nodded again.

Shannon waited, but it was obvious the only way she would get any more out of her patient was to keep asking questions. "Was this the first time you used?"

Gretchen shook her head. "Been using since the day after the last time I saw you. I was so angry at what you said that I used." Tears rolled down her cheeks.

"You can blame me all you want, but the choice to pick up a drug…that's on you."

"No, it's not. It's on you for telling me I can do better. And on my mother for sleeping with my new boyfriend."

"New boyfriend?" That was brand-new information. "You didn't tell me about the boyfriend. And we talked about how you need to stay away from your mother."

"My mom thinks you have a mommy complex with me," Gretchen said.

Shannon arched a brow. "I'm more concerned about how you feel about your mother sleeping with your new boyfriend."

"I had no idea he even knew my mom until I saw her coming out of his apartment. She had sex-hair, and his shirt wasn't tucked in. She grabbed his balls as she kissed him goodbye. I flipped."

Shannon reached for the tissue box and left it on the bed. Gretchen's mother had a record for prostitution, drugs, and she'd lost custody of her children when Gretchen was fourteen. Gretchen and her twin brother went to live with their father. Austin, her brother, died by suicide two years later. Gretchen was determined to follow in his footsteps. "So, you started using when you saw your mother and this boyfriend?" Shannon could understand how that would trigger the crazy thinking addicts used to justify picking up again after extended periods of sobriety.

Gretchen shook her head and then blew her nose. "I told you. I used when you said I could do better. When you judged my grades in school, my choice in friends, and wanting to have a relationship with my mother."

"Yes. I said you could do better because I know you tend to self-sabotage. But I've never judged you. As far as your mother is concerned—"

"Right. Make boundaries. Protect myself. I think I need protection from you." Gretchen paused to blow her nose again. "I hate her. She's the reason I'm like this. She's the reason I fell off the wagon. And I hate you because all you care about is keeping me sick. Making sure you get paid."

Shannon placed her hand gently on Gretchen's wrist.

Gretchen yanked her arm free.

"You will get through this. I believe in you." Shannon swallowed her lie. She wanted to have faith in Gretchen. Wanted to trust she'd be one of the few who truly changed the course of her life, but Shannon had her doubts.

Big doubts.

Gretchen would have to learn how to change and then like the person she chose to be.

The choice was always the hardest part.

"I'm tired. I want to sleep," Gretchen said, tossing the candy wrapper onto the floor.

Shannon knew anything she said at this point would fall on deaf ears. Gretchen needed some time to detox, and then Shannon might be able to break through her defenses once again.

Shannon stepped into the hallway, closing the curtain.

"That didn't go too well," Erica said.

"No. It didn't. I'm concerned she's coming off the drugs too hard. Can you get Dr. Franklin to check her blood levels and adjust medication if necessary? No reason to let the poor girl suffer when we can make the withdrawal easier."

"Oh, I don't know. I could never question Dr. Franklin."

Shannon let out a long sigh as she checked her watch. All she wanted to do was put her feet up and stare at Jackson's strong profile under a cool spring night in front of a fire.

"You're not questioning him. You're giving him a message." Shannon took a piece of paper from behind the nurses' station and scribbled instructions. "I know Dr. Wood is in the hospital tonight. I will get him to check on my patient. You can give this to both Wood and Dr. Franklin." She shoved a piece of paper at Erica. "Learn to stand up to the doctors. You stood up to me, but only because you fear Dr. Franklin. Don't ever be afraid to speak your mind. We can't do our jobs without nurses. In this situation, you spend more time with our patients than we do. I bet you noticed how agitated Gretchen has been."

"Yes. I noticed."

"Good. Now, keep me informed. I'm concerned about Gretchen."

Shannon knew she'd done everything she possibly could for Gretchen. Yet her patient had still landed herself in the psych ward.

On suicide watch.

That had to reflect poorly on her ability as a therapist.

Maybe she should cancel on Jackson tonight. Because the way she felt, she just might be willing to use him purely for what he offered as a man.

And that would be a trigger to a beast she wasn't sure she could tame.

CHAPTER FIVE

I f one thing had served Jackson well over the years, it was listening to his gut. Currently, his gut told him that things with the Montgomery case were not adding up to a girl on a vacation. He was glad that Janice, the roommate, had finally filed a missing person's report, and that the family had been notified—though they didn't seem to care all that much. They believed Belinda had fallen off the wagon and would show up the second she needed money.

According to Belinda's mother, Belinda had never been able to stay off drugs for more than a couple of months...except for this last year. She'd actually told Jackson that it was about time Belinda started using again. The hard part was that Jackson understood why Mrs. Montgomery would say such a horrible thing.

He sat in the parking lot of the Sagamore Hotel.

The white building overlooked the lake, much like the cover of the book, *The Shining*. The massive hotel filled the small island, giving the occupants a panoramic view of the lake set in the mountains' valley. During the day, the piece of property gleamed and ushered in relaxation. But he'd seen the hotel from a boat at night, and it screamed a tale of horror, imagined by little boys who'd seen *Halloween* one too many times.

The crew at the reception desk had been more forthcoming than Jackson had expected. That might have been because the police had already been by to ask questions, but according to the hotel records, Belinda hadn't been there at all.

Just as Jackson threw his truck into gear, his cell vibrated. "What's up, Katie?"

"Two things. First, I got a name on the new boyfriend for Belinda. Clayton Moosehead."

"Moosehead?" Odd name.

"Yeah, but when I searched, I got about thirty names locally. Most are either eighty-year-old men, dead, or don't live in the area anymore. Those who do, don't fit the description."

"Need to widen the search to the entire state." Jackson put the truck into park. "Who gave you the tip on the name?"

"One of the bank tellers. Ms. Timms was none too happy I was there, and I suspect she gave the teller a hard time. But, basically, the employee remembered the guy because he came in to cash a check and was all flirty. She said that Belinda walked him outside and gave him a wet one in the parking lot."

"A wet one? Is that new talk for blow—"

"Jesus, get your mind out of the gutter. A kiss. You know? Sucking face. Making out."

Jackson laughed. "Anything else?" He hit the speaker button, placed the cell in the hands-free cradle, and pulled out onto Route 9, heading south. It wouldn't take more than ten minutes to get home. He was tired and hungry and had a sudden need to throw a couple of hamburgers on the grill.

That was if Shannon hadn't eaten already.

"No," Katie said flatly. "But I also talked with Ben again and asked him if he knew this guy, Clayton. He told me that Clayton was a freelance photographer or something, and that Belinda had some nudes taken. She told him it was a gift for him, but not until after he'd gotten jealous and freaked out on her."

"Nice," Jackson said.

"Pig."

"I act like a guy; you call me a pig. I put flowers on your desk; you call me a girl. I can't win with you."

"Well, maybe you can win with the shrink."

"She's not a shrink," he said under his breath.

"Aren't you touchy?" Katie said. "I'm going to do some more digging when I get home and see what I can find. Before I forget, the package you requested about Shannon's daughter arrived. I haven't opened it."

"Feel like swinging it by my place?" He knew the information in the packet wouldn't tell him where Shannon's daughter had ended up or her name, but it would match non-identifying information and give him a start. He figured he'd be able to give Shannon some peace of mind in a week or so.

At least, he hoped the news would be good, and that Shannon would let her daughter go through life with the loving parents she'd been placed with and not insert herself into their lives, disrupting their family dynamic.

A surge of hot pain rushed through his body. Shannon was nothing like his birth mother. He shouldn't compare the two.

But, still, certain skeletons were sometimes best left locked in the closet.

"I'm in your driveway," Katie said.

"Thanks. I'll be there shortly if you want to hang out for a bit." Well, his sisters certainly would be pleased by his hospitality, but he wished he hadn't uttered the words. He wanted some alone time with Shannon. One of these days, he hoped they would move past neighborly conversation and into something different. Something more.

Something that might make his mother and his sisters happy.

But he'd be lying to himself if he didn't have reservations, regardless of his attraction. It had nothing to do with Shannon giving up a child and everything to do with her wanting to find that child.

"Wish I could. I'm going to meet with Jacob's dad about my uncle's case. No way do I want that man out of jail, but something tells me he might actually make parole this time," Katie said, the words tumbling out of her mouth like a volcano. "I used my key and left it on your desk."

"Perfect. Thanks. I'll see you in the morning." Jackson ended the call. He navigated his way down the long, dark road, his mind heavy with thoughts he'd long forgotten.

His parents and sisters had always told him that blood didn't make a family.

And they were right. People even thought that he and his sisters looked alike, but none of them had the same DNA.

Jackson slowed at the top of his driveway. The light blue sedan was long gone, but as he rolled slowly down toward his cottage on the lake, he noticed a pricy BMW in Shannon's space.

But Shannon's car was nowhere to be found.

He pulled in and made his way toward the side of his cabin. He always thought it strange that these particular properties only had one entrance, located on the side of the house. They were small domiciles, Cape Cod-style, but not so small they couldn't support a front and back door. However, for security reasons, he liked having only one way in and out.

He hadn't taken ten steps when two women came barreling around the corner.

"Oh," the older woman said. "You're not Shannon."

"Nope," Jackson said, seeing the resemblance immediately between the older woman and Shannon. They both had striking blue eyes and sandy brown hair. The older woman wore way too much makeup and dressed as if she were the first lady, but otherwise, she looked very much like Shannon. "Name's Jackson."

"Yes," the woman said. "I'm Shannon's mother, Melinda. And this is my daughter, Tara. I was hoping Shannon might be home by now." Melinda checked her watch. "I need to head back to Saratoga, but Tara here," she paused, glancing at the young girl, "she was planning a girls' night with her sister, and her car is in the shop so I agreed to drive her." Melinda tapped her watch. "Wonder what could be keeping Shannon."

"I wasn't planning anything," Tara said. "I thought this was—"

"She's always late," Melinda said. "Maybe Jackson here can keep you company until Shannon gets home?"

Before Jackson could say anything, Melinda nearly sprinted toward her car.

"See you tomorrow." She glanced over her shoulder and blew a kiss. "You two have a pleasant evening. You know, it's such a beautiful night. You should walk down to the waterfront and watch the moon and stars come out while you wait for Shannon. Yes. Go now." She waved to them as she slipped into her car.

Cue music for The Twilight Zone, Jackson thought. He turned and glanced at Tara, who appeared just as shocked as he felt. Tara had Shannon's eyes, but otherwise, they didn't look that much alike. Tara was tiny compared to Shannon's lush curves. Tara had to be at least four inches shorter than her sister. Even though her jet-black hair didn't show roots of another color, having five sisters, he could tell a dye job a mile away.

He tried to picture the girl with light brown hair, and as he did, he knew he'd seen her somewhere before. "You look familiar."

"You're the PI guy that works with Katie, right?"

He nodded.

"Yeah. You might have seen me in your building. My boyfriend is Kevin Bengal."

"Oh, yeah. I do work for him and his father's law firm. Nice guy."

"Too bad our parents can't stay the fuck out of our lives. Unbelievable. I hope Shannon gets home soon," Tara said. She tapped her phone then put it next to her ear. "Oh, come on, Mom. I know you have your phone turned on. Pick it up."

Jackson stood there, hands on his hips, trying to figure out what to say. But his mind was devoid of words.

Tara groaned and banged on her cell with her index finger. Damn thing might break if she kept that up.

"It's cool. You don't have to babysit me. I'll just hang

out on the patio until Shannon gets back or until I get my mother to turn around."

Well, that didn't explain much. "I'm a little confused. Your sister didn't tell me you were coming, and she and I were supposed to have drinks." He cringed. If his mother were here, she'd slap the back of his head for being so rude.

Tara glanced in his direction and smirked. "Seriously? My sister finally said yes to a date with you?"

He cleared his throat.

"Sorry. It's just that Cameron talks about you all the time."

"Who's that?"

"Shannon's best friend from college. Anyway, I'll be out of your hair shortly," Tara said. "My mother kind of lives in her own world and, unfortunately, you just entered her orbit unwillingly. Worst case, I call an Uber."

"Is her world a really bad place to be?" Jackson asked, his inquisitive side taking over. He'd get over the tiny ounce of guilt he felt scratching his mind over pumping Tara for information.

But first, he'd have to get her to stick with one subject at a time.

Tara laughed. "Not usually for me. My sister is a different story. And today, you are her pawn."

"Do I want to know why?"

Tara took in a deep breath. "Long story short, I

made the mistake of not being aware that my mother was lurking in the shadows when I got into a tiff with my boyfriend. We both said some things we shouldn't have, but his father and my mother are making us both nuts. I told him I needed to cool off, and he said he needed a break. I think my mom took that as us breaking up—which we didn't. Then she told me that Shannon was having a hard time because yesterday was the anniversary of her father's death. Which I should have known was total bullshit, but I fell for it because I love my sister and would do anything for her."

"Is there a conclusion to this story?" Jackson was concerned the girl would pass out if she didn't take a breath.

"Oh. Yeah. I think my mother plans to inform Kevin that I'm spending the evening with you to try and make him jealous."

Jackson squeezed his hand into a tight fist before shaking it out. "I hope your boyfriend is smarter than that."

"He is. But that doesn't change the rumors my mother could spread in her dainty little group of gossiping control freaks who have way too much time on their hands."

"Want a soda? Or maybe a beer or something?" Jackson asked. His sisters would be disappointed if he didn't show the young lady some hospitality. And, since Tara was so willing to rattle things off, he figured she might give him some insight into Shannon. "You are old enough to drink, aren't you?"

"I'm twenty-two, thank you very much. And I'd love a drink. If you have wine, I'd prefer that. But no biggie if you don't. Just anything with alcohol in it. I'm going to need it to calm myself down so I don't strangle my mother, the meddling pain in the ass."

"Why don't you sit here?" He pointed to the chairs around the fire pit. "Mine are better than your sister's. She really needs to get wooden ones."

"No, shit."

Jackson enjoyed Tara's sassy personality. It reminded him of his sister, Sarah. "I've got a phone call to make. But when I'm done, I'll bring out a bottle of wine."

"Perfect," she said, her focus back on her cell.

He unlocked his front door and then flew up the stairs, taking the steps two at a time. As soon as he was at the top, he pulled out his phone and dialed Shannon's number. He wanted to make sure Tara didn't hear a word of the conversation.

She answered on the second ring. "Hello?"

"It's Jackson. Just thought you might like to know your mother stopped by."

"To see you?"

"Not sure, she left in a hurry. But she also left your sister, Tara, behind for me to entertain."

"Well, shit. I'm so sorry," Shannon said. "What did my mother say?"

"Not much, but your sister's rambling on and on, and I'm confused about a few things."

"I'm not surprised. She's a talker, like my mother. Thankfully, she doesn't meddle in everyone else's business, even though she has an opinion about everything. I'll be home in ten minutes or so, depending on traffic."

"I'll keep your sister amused. Or maybe it will be the other way around." Jackson put his phone into his pocket.

He snagged a nice bottle of red and three glasses.

Tara had made herself comfortable in one of the chairs and kicked her feet up onto one of the end tables. "Thank you." She grabbed the glass he offered and took a generous sip. "I'm going to wait for my sister. I'd like to talk to her for a couple of minutes, but then I'll leave so you can have your date."

"It wasn't a date, really. We sometimes share an evening drink or have a morning cup of coffee."

Tara tipped her head, raising her eyelids to give him a sideways glance. "Are you implying you roll out of bed and drink coffee with my sister? Which house do you sleep at?"

Jackson felt his cheeks flush. "I didn't mean it that way."

Tara laughed, waving her hand in the air. "I know. My sister doesn't do relationships. Not even sure she's ever had a one-night stand, much less let a man spend the night. Cameron and I have tried fixing her up a dozen times. Shannon always finds a reason to end something before it even starts. Something about her job being too time-consuming and sucking up all her emotional energy or some such bullshit."

Jackson tossed a few pieces of wood into the pit and shoved a wad of newspaper under them before lighting a fire stick. He'd been gun-shy for the last year. Divorce tended to do that to a man. But he hadn't given up on the idea of finding the right woman.

It sounded like Shannon didn't even want to consider spending her life with anyone, and that had his mind turning over a million questions about why.

There was always a reason.

"She just hasn't found the right man, that's all," Jackson said.

The wood crackled as the fire took hold, sending sparks and smoke into the sky. He eased into the chair with the best view of the road, something he never did. He always preferred to stare at the dark water lapping at the shore. But tonight, he only wanted to watch Shannon park her car and join him.

"The problem is, she doesn't even look. I swear she dates a guy for a couple of weeks and only when we have family stuff going on. Then, all of a sudden, he's gone. We're all wondering who she'll bring to Bonnie's wedding. Did she ask you?"

"Who's Bonnie?"

Tara laughed. "Wow. You know almost nothing about Shannon."

"Sadly, that's true," he admitted, tipping his glass. "I wouldn't mind changing that."

"Good luck. And to answer your question, Bonnie is my other sister."

"Older or younger?"

"She's Shannon's age. Actually, they are only a few months apart." Tara smiled.

"How is that possible?"

"They are both my half-sisters. Bonnie and I have the same father. Shannon and I have the same mother. Bonnie is Shannon's stepsister. None of us have a whole sister."

Jackson burst out laughing. Tara was certainly a firecracker. "I have five whole sisters. Trust me, it's overrated."

"Wow. You poor man, surrounded by all that estrogen. My father always says it's going to put him six feet under long before he's ready. When we were younger, we all loved sending him to the store for tampons, and we all wanted different brands and styles."

"I never needed to know that." Jackson pointed to the car making its way down the long, windy driveway. "Here comes your sister." Thank God. As much as Jackson enjoyed Tara, he was ready for conversations with a different flavor.

"Hey," Shannon said, dropping her purse onto the chair next to Jackson. "Sorry our mother dragged you into her games."

"No worries." Jackson stood, handing her a glass.

"Why don't I leave you two alone for a bit? But I do need to talk to you about a couple of things before the night ends."

"I'll knock on the door when we're done."

Jackson slipped into his kitchen, glancing over his shoulder. He'd gotten nothing specific out of Tara about Shannon, but what he had learned made him pause. Every family had its fair share of dysfunction—including his. But he wasn't sure he wanted to get involved with a woman whose mother would go to such lengths to interfere with her adult children's lives.

———

"I'm so sorry, sis."

"You should be." Shannon adjusted her chair a little closer to the fire. The evening air had chilled her bones, and the day she'd had warranted the five gulps of wine she swallowed without even tasting it. "Curious. When did Mother decide to come here for a visit, and what was the reason she gave you?" She tossed a piece of paper she'd found wadded up in her pocket into the fire. "And why the hell did you believe her?"

"I know you're upset, but you don't have to take that tone with me. I didn't do anything wrong," Tara said. "You know how Mother gets."

Shannon dropped her head to the back of the chair. "I know. I'm just tired. I had a bad day at work, and Mom has been a pain in the ass. And *your* other sister is more like *our* mother than we are. I've gotten ten texts from her today. If she's so afraid I'll ruin her fucking bridal party, why the hell did she ask me to be in the wedding in the first place?"

"To appease my dad. He always feels like you get the short end of the stick, and I'd have to agree."

"Your father is a saint."

"Amen to that, sister." Tara raised her glass. "Mom said she was worried about you when she saw you yesterday. That should have been my first clue. But, honestly, sometimes you do get weird on the day your dad died. I know you don't like to talk about him, but it's not like I don't know some of what happened."

"You were only four years old when he died, and you only met the man a few times."

"Yeah, but I lived with you, and I remember the bruises. I recall once listening to him tell Mom that you got drunk and fell down the stairs and that she should ground you."

"I was drunk, but he pushed me," Shannon admitted, letting out a long sigh. "I wish you didn't remember those things. That had to be scary for you." She had opened up to her little sister about some of the abuse because she felt she had to, but she'd kept the worst of it to herself.

Her father was dead. The skeletons were safely tucked away in the closet. There was no point.

"It was at times. But, honestly, I only have a couple of memories like that. Why doesn't Mom want to admit what happened?" Tara asked. Her voice trembled as she wiped a tear from her cheek. "There are some things about our mother I will never understand."

"Did Mom do something else?"

Tara shook her head. "Other than being a crazed psycho about Bonnie's wedding and being a little weirder than usual about the anniversary of your dad's death, no."

"Weird how?"

"Yesterday, she started bringing up you and all your problems and what it did to her and my dad, as if that's what caused your dad's death."

If Tara only knew the half of it. "We can't forget that I didn't make it easy on Mom or your dad. I was popping pills, doing coke, getting in all sorts of trouble. Mom was terrified of me, and your dad wanted to protect you." Shannon lifted her feather pendant. When she'd gotten pregnant, her mother had sent her off to a halfway house and told her stepsister that she'd gone to rehab. That wasn't true. And when she'd come home, she'd gone right back into the insanity of the drug scene.

Of course, her father had helped perpetuate that lie.

But poor Tara had thought Shannon had gone to boarding school, and Shannon would never forget the day she left, listing to Tara scream and cry for her not to go.

"I wish I could have done something." Tara sipped her wine.

127

"You were a child, and it was a long time ago. Let's get back to our current predicament."

"Right. Mom thought it would be good if I surprised you. I hadn't seen you in a while, so I thought that would be fun. She insisted on driving and assured me you were excited and couldn't wait to see me."

"Since when are you and I incapable of making our own arrangements?"

"Since never. But you've been withdrawn lately."

Shannon pursed her lips. "So have you. And Mom told me about her crazy plan to make Kevin jealous. Why the hell did the two of you break up?"

"We didn't. We just got into a fight, and we both agreed we needed to cool off." Tara stood, walking in a circle around the fire, twirling her dark hair.

"I don't get how she thinks this will work," Tara said. "First of all, Kevin doesn't get jealous. And second, we just took a break from each other. He needed some space after the big fight about his potential new job, so we really haven't called it splitsville. We're just taking a week to think about what we really want and what that means."

"Wait. Step back. Kevin got offered a job? But he works for his dad."

"His father is almost as controlling as Mom. Kevin doesn't want to be a criminal lawyer, and he got offered a job in Newburgh in the district attorney's office. He wants to take it."

"How do you feel about that?"

"I'm fine with it. I've even put in applications for a couple of schools, but it's what he did when he told me he took the job that freaked me right the fuck out."

"Dare I ask?" Shannon loved her little sister, but her dramatics often grated on her nerves.

"He proposed."

"He *what*?" Shannon asked, dropping her glass, red wine splattering across her pant leg. Thankfully, the glass didn't shatter when it hit the grass, but her pants turned a dark red. "Shit." She kicked her foot, rubbing her hand over her slacks.

"Only you, sis."

Shannon laughed, pouring more wine. "Did you say yes?"

"Yes, and no. He wants to run off to Vegas. It's not that I have a problem doing that, but both sets of parents would disown us. I can take Mom being a basket case, but I couldn't handle both sets of parents being upset."

"They'd get over it. But the real question is, do you want a big wedding?"

Tara laughed. "Good God, no. If you think Bonnie's wedding is outrageous, imagine what it would be like with Melinda Cartwright and Charlene Bangal as event coordinators. Kevin and I'd be lost, and it wouldn't even be about us. It'd be about them."

"Then I don't get it. What's the problem? Elope and deal with the shitstorm later. Unless the move is the issue."

Tara let out a long sigh. "No. I could get used to anywhere as long as I'm with Kevin, but it all came on so fast." Tara smiled. "He wants to do it in two months after Bonnie's wedding. And since he took the job, we'd be moving about the same time."

"I still don't get the problem."

"Besides, he hasn't told his father about not working for him anymore. I'm more worried about how his parents will take the elopement and him moving all at once. Mom has Dad to help her get over it, and Bonnie always has to be the center of attention, giving our mom something to focus on. But Kevin is an only child, and it will crush his dad."

Shannon put her hand on Tara's and squeezed. "You and Kevin have to start setting boundaries when it comes to your parents. If they want to have a relationship with you, then they will come around. Hell, even our mom has gotten better over the years when it comes to me because I don't let her rule my life."

"I know. I know." Tara tossed her hands wide.

"So, does that mean you're going to go track down Kevin and tell him you'll run off and never look back?"

"I think that's a great idea." Tara snagged her cell from the plastic table. "Holy shit."

"What is it?"

"I've got five texts that say he's on his way here."

"Well, his timing is perfect." Shannon pointed to the car headed down the driveway. "Call me later, okay?"

Tara jumped from her seat and smoothed down her miniskirt. "I love you, sis."

"Right back at you."

Shannon pulled Tara in for a hug. She held her longer than usual. She'd never been a touchy-feely kind of girl, but it was time she started making some changes in her life and being a better sister was a good place to start. "Let's have lunch one day next week. Just the two of us."

"I'd like that."

Shannon wrapped her arms around her middle as she watched her sister leap into Kevin's arms. She smiled as the young couple kissed passionately. In spite of their mother, Tara had grown up well, and Shannon was thrilled that she and Kevin would be getting out of their parents' grips and living their lives.

Their way.

She fingered the pendant hanging from her neck.

Freedom.

She turned and stared at the *Sweet Freedom* rocking gently in the dark waters of Lake George. The moon cast a glow on the tall mast. There was a time in her life when Shannon enjoyed being on the water and feeling the wind in her face. The feeling when the captain cut the engine, the sails filled, heeling, making the boat take flight across the water.

"You're deep in thought," Jackson said as he looped his arm around her waist.

She jumped, knocking his beer out of his hand. It

flipped and sizzled, spewing the liquid over the fire and him. "Shit. I hate it when people sneak up on me."

He took a step back, holding his hands to the air. "Sorry. I assumed you heard my door slam shut."

"Please, just don't do that to me again."

"Don't worry, I won't. Now, do you want to sit out here by the fire and talk or go inside?"

She deserved his curtness and then some. The only excuse she had was the day had been long and hard, and all she really wanted was a hot bath and another glass of wine.

"Out here is good."

"All right. Let me get myself another beer." As if he'd read her mind, he lifted her wine glass and filled it. "Need a blanket?"

She nodded, curling her fingers around his muscular biceps. "I'm sorry. I could list a plethora of excuses for my behavior—"

He pressed his finger over her lips. "It's okay. I was rude, and I'm sorry, too. Give me five minutes."

Dropping her hand, she blinked, trying to break his searing stare. He looked at her with forgiveness behind his dark, questioning eyes. It was if she were the only thing that mattered. She swallowed. Being the center of attention hadn't ever been something she desired. If anything, she preferred to be a wallflower.

He ran his finger over her cheek.

Her chest heaved as she tried to take a deep breath.

"I think it's you who's the enigma," he whispered, right before he pressed his hot lips over her mouth.

For a second, every muscle tensed into a tight ball of nerves. She gripped his shirt, needing to push him away but wanting to draw him closer. Her brain screamed at her that getting involved with him romantically would only end with one of them getting hurt.

Probably, her hurting him.

However, as his tongue slipped between her lips, and her body relaxed into his, she realized that he could break her heart if she let him in too deeply. He was the kind of man little girls dreamed of marrying, and grown-up women searched for in all the wrong places.

"Jackson," she said, prying her mouth from his. She rested her hands on his chest. "Where did that come from?"

He arched a brow. "You don't think it's been brewing for a while?"

In all her adult life, no liaison she'd ever had with a man had percolated. There had been maybe four men that she could have considered herself being in a relationship with, and all of them had been superficial. The last one, Jared, a man she'd met in her PhD program, had been sweet and kind, and he had a huge heart, but she could never truly give herself to him. And after nearly a year, he'd called it quits. Last she'd heard, he'd gotten engaged a few months ago.

"I've spent most of my life buried in schoolwork

and then defending my dissertation and building my career. Having a man in my life hasn't been a priority."

"What does that have to do with the fact that we're attracted to each other now."

She opened her mouth but snapped it shut.

"I'd like to take you out on a real date."

"My stepsister is getting married in two weeks, would you like to go with me?"

He arched a brow. "I'd love to."

"I was kidding."

"I'm not. I'd enjoy it. Now, let me get myself a beer, and then I need to change the subject to business."

"Sounds like a plan. But before we do that, I need to make something clear. I'm going solo to my sister's wedding. I shouldn't have joked about that. My family is insane, if you haven't noticed."

"I'll hold the date, just in case you change your mind." He turned and headed toward the door.

She watched his ass flex against the fabric of his pants that clung to him like a wetsuit, detailing every muscle. Letting out an audible sigh, she eased into the chair and poked the fire with a stick. The flames snapped like fireflies toward the star-filled sky.

She dropped her head back and closed her eyes, focusing on the sounds of the evening—the cars revving on the street above. Boat engines humming on the lake below. Anything to get Jackson out of her head.

"I'm coming out of the house now," Jackson called.

"Thanks for the heads-up." She waved her hand over the chair as if she were giving him the white flag of surrender.

"I need to ask you some questions about the adoption. I probably should have had you come into the office versus ruining the ambiance here—"

"I spend all day in an office. If you don't mind, I'd prefer to discuss this anywhere but your place of work."

"I can respect that," he said, holding a packet of papers on his lap. "I've got all the un-identifying information on you and your daughter."

"What does that mean?"

"It has all of your medical information at the time of the adoption. It's the history you provided to the hospital about family, and a write-up about your general appearance, race, religion, as taken at the time of the adoption."

"I don't think I've ever seen that." She took the papers he handed and flipped through them.

"You wouldn't. But it's given to the adoptive parents and then sits in the registry. If anyone comes looking for you, the father, or the child, the records get pinged."

She dropped the document. The breeze kicked up, taking it into the fire. "Shit."

"I've got another copy," Jackson said. "Are you always this klutzy?"

"I am." She swallowed. "Can you tell if my daughter came looking for me?"

"That's the beauty of a closed adoption. It protects both party's privacy but allows for a mutual meeting."

"Jesus Christ. Will you just answer my question?"

"I'm trying," he said, slipping on a pair of eyeglasses, letting them rest on the bridge of his nose. "New York State uses a confidential intermediary program. If your daughter went looking for you, then once you enter the registry, she will be notified and be given whatever information you consented to."

"I really don't want to interrupt her life. And I don't want to meet her. So, is there a way to locate her without sending up a smoke signal?"

"That would be a lot harder and costly. You don't have to give your contact information on the registry. But you will have to give full birth name and proof of the adoption."

"You have the birth certificate they gave me before the adoption."

He nodded. "You named her Carly. Was there a reason for the name?"

"It means a woman who has her freedom," she said, turning her head. The tears stung the corners of her dry eyes.

"Did you know that when you gave it to her?"

She nodded.

"I guess now I understand why you didn't like my boat's name."

He hadn't a clue, and he never would. "I know it's not really her name. She's probably never heard it before." Shannon clutched her necklace. Her heart filled her chest with one pounding beat after the other.

"Are you okay?" His warm hand squeezed her knee.

"It's been a long time since I heard the name I gave her, much less talked about that time in my life." She swiped at her cheeks. "This is harder than I thought it would be."

"Do you want to stop?"

"No. I need to know."

"All right. What about her father? You have him listed as unknown."

She let out a sarcastic laugh. "And you think I lied about that."

"I didn't say that. But it's one more avenue to go looking for her."

"Well, I honestly don't know who the father is. Go ahead, judge that." The shame, guilt, rage, and confusion billowed to the surface like a tree being yanked from the ground during a tornado.

"You need to stop that. There is no room for me taking your inventory in this case. I agreed to do this for you because I believe in you and your reasons. Now, if you want to make my job a little easier, could you tell me who the potential father could be?"

"It doesn't matter. No one but my parents knew I was pregnant. Not even the boys I'd been sleeping with."

"You can't be totally sure of that."

"I can be, and unless you can't find her at all

without that information, which I highly doubt, I'd rather not utter those names."

Ted Ratler.

Alex Angler.

Chad Roaming.

Rodger Williams.

Borden Cox.

She'd never forget their names. Their faces. Their laughter.

The hair on the back of her neck prickled as if the Tartan boat grew a pair of eyes and stared her down. They'd all been adults. Even Borden and Alex, who were both barely twenty-one at the time. Still, they should have known better.

They were all drunk and high on coke, but that didn't mean she'd consented.

Or that the men hadn't paid her father in some way for her *services*.

"This is hard for me because I consider you a friend, so I wouldn't normally ask this question." He rubbed the back of his neck. "Do you want to talk about what happened?" His sweet voice glided over her old wounds like a medicated Band-Aid.

"There's nothing to talk about." She smiled. "It's just a lot of stuff I haven't thought about in a long time. I'd rather not be in that registry or contact who might be the father. So, if there are other ways to find out where she is, I'd like to do that. I'm not worried about the cost at the moment."

"It's going to take time."

"I've waited nearly nineteen years. I can wait a little while longer."

"I'll do my best. Now, I have one other thing I need to discuss with you. Do you remember that car that has been parked at the top of the hill most mornings?"

She nodded.

"Well, it's registered to Ned Brendel."

"No way," she said. It was an interesting turn of events, and she wasn't sure if she should be scared shitless or flattered that dear old Uncle Ned gave a crap. "I take it you know he's my uncle."

"Yeah," he said. "Why is he spying on you?"

She untucked her feet and slipped them back into her shoes. "I honestly have no idea," she said. "I haven't spoken to him since my father died."

Jackson scribbled on a notepad. She tried to peer over his strong biceps, but she couldn't make out the words. "Why not?"

She didn't need him digging more into her personal life. Looking for her daughter was crazy enough. Bringing the Brendel brand of crazy would be beyond insane.

"I'm not close with anyone on my father's side of the family."

Jackson glanced over the rims of his glasses. "Can you elaborate?"

"Like I said, my dad wasn't a nice guy, and his

family knew it. My uncle Ned has tried to reach out a few times this last year, but I haven't responded."

"That really doesn't explain the snooping."

No, it didn't, and she'd be lying if it didn't cause some concern. But she wasn't about to discuss it with Jackson. That part of her life didn't need to creep into her present.

Not ever.

"Mind if I give him a call? Ask him a few questions?"

"I kind of mind." She raised her hand, chewing on her fingernail. "My uncle has a gambling problem—among other things. I'm sure he's just looking for a handout."

"That makes me worry he'd break into your home if he thinks you have something of value."

"Can you call him without mentioning me?"

"I can absolutely do that." Jackson took his reading glasses off and set them on the stack of papers he'd tossed on the table. "I think that concludes the business portion of the evening." He gripped the armrests and hoisted himself closer.

"What are you doing?" she asked with a nervous laugh.

"I have this rule. Never mix business with pleasure." He continued captivating her with his wicked smile and playful eyes. It felt as though he were holding her in his arms, even though he was a few feet away.

"It's a good rule." She tore her gaze away. No matter

how attractive she found him, she needed to take a step back. Getting involved with him would only cause problems for both of them. "I have the same one."

He stood and reached out his hand. She hesitated for a brief moment, and before she knew it, he had his hands on her hips and his lips on her cheek. "I really like you," he whispered.

She took a step back and swallowed. "I like you, too, but I don't think this is a good idea, especially with the blending of two cases."

"I don't like the voice of reason." He cocked his head and frowned.

"You're a nice man, and I do enjoy your company, but—"

He hushed her by pressing his soft lips to her mouth.

She leaned in to his strong frame and moaned. She couldn't believe she caved so quickly to his tender touch. She'd never met a man who had such a physical and emotional effect on her, and she wasn't used to it. She didn't know how to control her emotions.

She pressed her hand against his chest. "You're really good at that."

"You're not so bad yourself." He winked.

"It's getting late, and I have early appointments."

He took her chin between his thumb and forefinger. "Can I cook you dinner tomorrow after work?"

"I'd like that."

"Good night, Shannon."

"Good night." She turned on a dime and scurried across the yard. She didn't glance over her shoulder. After closing the door and locking it, she leaned against the wooden frame, fiddling with her necklace.

Her cell buzzed in her back pocket. She pulled it out and smiled at Jackson's smiley face text.

Her life was really finally coming together.

CHAPTER SIX

Jackson's phone rang out, jostling him from a deep sleep. He stretched, rolling to his side.

At two in the morning, it had to be Katie, even though he wished it was Shannon asking him to sneak over for the night.

He snagged the cell and tapped the screen. "This'd better be good. I was right in the middle of an amazing dream."

"Belinda Montgomery is dead," Katie's voice boomed across the room, bouncing off the walls. "They found her body on Long Island."

He bolted to an upright position. "No fucking way."

"Yep. I'm on my way to get you by boat."

"You don't own a boat." He shoved the covers to the side and searched for his jeans.

"I borrowed Jacob's. Be at the dock in fifteen."

"On it." He hiked up his pants, found a sweatshirt,

143

and made his way down toward the dock, rubbing the sleep from his eyes. He glanced over his shoulder. Shannon's cottage was dark. He thought about texting her, but he'd wait until he knew more.

Breaking other people's rules was something Jackson rarely thought twice about. Breaking *his* rules, well...he created them for a reason.

But Shannon Brendel and her sexy legs that went on forever had been torturing him in his dreams for months. Their early-morning conversations hadn't been anything deep. More like casual chatter one would expect between neighbors. But they affected him to his core, making him willing to toss caution to the wind.

He stood on the dock in front of his cottage, staring at a white light moving across the lake.

The boat engine got louder. He glanced over his shoulder. Hopefully, he'd be back before Shannon left for work in the morning.

Katie pulled up to the dock in a small Boston Whaler. Jackson stepped aboard and then pushed it from the dock.

"Wow. That sailboat is something else," Katie said as she pushed the throttle forward. "I still think you should send a picture of it to your ex-wife and tell her you bought it with the money from the divorce settlement."

"I'd rather not have any contact with her, thank you," Jackson said. His marriage ranked right up there as the biggest mistake of his life, and one he didn't like discussing.

With anyone.

It was over, and she was out of his life.

"You could be sipping tropical drinks in the Bahamas had you gone after her."

"Life isn't always about money. Besides, if you'd met her, you'd be wondering why the hell I married her in the first place." He stuffed his hands into his pockets. "What do you know about this case?"

"A young couple found Belinda's body under a picnic table at the campsite next to them. I guess they were a little intoxicated and went to the wrong site. Took Lake George patrol fifteen minutes to get there."

"So, State is taking point?"

"Don't know. Westerfield is on-site now, and I'm sure he wants jurisdiction, but it doesn't affect us one way or the other."

Jackson stood next to the center console on Katie's side of the boat. Katie pulled back on the throttle as they approached the five-mile-an-hour buoys between Long Island and Assembly Point. "They aren't going to let us anywhere near the scene."

"Probably not," she agreed. "But just driving by, we'll be able to tell if they are considering it a suicide, overdose, or murder."

"You already think it's murder, don't you?"

"I don't know what to think. This case gets weirder

145

and weirder by the second. But once we get confirmation that she's dead, our case is technically over."

Katie navigated the boat through the buoys and then pulled in tight to the shoreline of the island. Jackson could see the lights about twenty campsites up ahead. There appeared to be two LG patrol boats, a sheriff's department boat, and a fire rescue boat. A helicopter buzzed overhead with a spotlight—they were looking for something...or someone.

"Call Westerfield," Katie said. "He's knows we're out here."

Jackson pulled up his contact information.

"Westerfield here."

"What's going on?" Jackson asked.

"Hang on," Westerfield said. A brief moment passed. "Treating it as a homicide. There are a ton of bruises on the girl's body, and we don't think this is where she died."

"What about the new boyfriend we were told she was with?"

"No sign of him, but we have people looking."

"What's going to happen if we drive close?" Jackson asked.

"As long as you stay a good fifty feet from the island, we won't do anything. I'll call you when I wrap up here."

Jackson tapped Katie on the shoulder and made one gesture toward the patrol boats and then indicated for them to go out a little ways. "All right," Jackson said. "Talk to you soon."

"So?" Katie asked.

"Increase speed to about ten miles per hour and drive out about fifty feet from shore. I get the feeling Westerfield is keeping something from us. Not sure what, but whatever it is, I bet we'll see it if we look hard enough."

Katie punched the throttle. Even with all the lights, the campsite was hard to see through the lush trees and the people milling about.

Jackson shivered. Who went camping in April when the night dipped well into the forties? "Slow down," he said as he maneuvered around to the other side of the boat. A flag floating in the water over an innertube caught his attention. "There are divers in the water." He pointed. "And that's a New York State Trooper SCUBA team boat."

"I see it. Another body, maybe?"

"Could be. I can't imagine a woman coming out here in April alone. Besides, we still have the new boyfriend that no one can find."

"Could be a double homicide. Or maybe a murder-suicide case. Either way, if that's our girl, our job is done," Katie repeated.

"We might as well go home and wait for confirmation." Jackson sat down next to Katie. He had no idea how he was going to tell Shannon. The even bigger question was whether he should wake her up tonight. He glanced at his watch—three in the morning.

He should wait. But for how long? If the cops released any information, it would hit the news pretty quickly, and Shannon was the kind of woman who paid attention to the news.

Katie kept the boat at a low speed as they maneuvered around Long Island and headed back toward Jackson's place.

"Before I forget, I got a call from Bengal. He's got a couple of new cases for us."

"Funny. I met the son's girlfriend earlier. She happens to be Shannon's half-sister."

"Small world," Katie said. "Bengal's kid doesn't want anything to do with working for his father."

"How do you know that?"

"He's been spending a lot of time talking with Jacob about being an ADA."

"I'd rather do work for the DA's office, but we need the money." One thing he'd learned over the last year was that he couldn't always pick and choose his cases. He no longer had a rich wife.

Thank God. Not that he hadn't enjoyed the money. That said, living with her had turned out to be pure hell. And that was before she'd broken his heart by cheating on him while he was in the hospital after nearly dying from a gunshot wound.

"Thank Jacob for the use of the boat," he said as he jumped onto the dock.

"He doesn't know I borrowed it."

Jackson should be shocked, but it was a typical Katie move. "Great. We just stole the assistant district attorney's boat," Jackson said and then pushed the bow. "See you in the morning." The moment he turned, he noticed that Shannon's lights were on. He started to head up the stone path to her cottage when the door flew open. Shannon raced toward the side of the house in jeans and a long sweater. Her hair looked as if she'd spent the day on a motorcycle going a hundred miles an hour without a helmet.

"Shannon," he yelled. "Wait."

She gasped, skidding to a halt. "Shit, Jackson. You scared me. I'm sorry. I've got to run. Some problems at work."

"I'm sorry about your patient," he said as he jogged to where she stood.

She tilted her head and wrinkled her nose with a puzzled look. "How did you know?"

"Katie called, and we drove up to Long Island to check it out. It looks like they are treating this as a suspicious death."

Shannon's eyes narrowed. "On Long Island? I'm sorry, but I don't follow. I've got a crisis at Saratoga Hospital, not Long Island."

"Oh, shit." Jackson scratched the back of his head. "I thought you knew I was talking about Belinda. They found her body at a campsite. I'm so sorry."

"Oh, God." Shannon took in a long, deep breath as

she braced herself against the side of the cottage. "Jesus. That's terrible." She breathed in and out slowly and methodically. "What happened?" she asked.

Gently, he ran his hand up and down her arm. "We don't really know. The police are investigating."

She stiffened her back. "I'm not going to wait for the police to come to me," she said. "Do you know who I should contact?"

"I don't know if the sheriff's office or the State Troopers are running point, but I can find out and let you know by mid-morning."

"I'd appreciate that." She fiddled with the key remote and unlocked her car. "I've got to get going. I've got a crisis in Saratoga. Call my cell, okay?"

"Sure thing." He wrapped his arms around her waist. "You're trembling."

"I have another patient in crisis. It's a lot to handle right now."

"What can I do for you?"

"Keep me in the loop about Belinda?"

He pressed his lips against her forehead. "I can do that."

"I really have to get going."

"Do me a favor and text me when you get to the hospital." He took a chance and stole a quick but passionate kiss before watching her race up the path and hop into her vehicle.

When his divorce had become final, he'd sworn off women.

After kissing Shannon, he decided to amend that statement and make it just rich women.

———

Shannon pushed open the doors toward the holding tank and raced through the hallways, her heart pounding against her chest.

"Hey, Kent," she said at the main doors.

Kent had been the one who called. He had sounded shaken but assured her that he was just fine. He gave her weak smile and nodded somberly.

"How are you holding up?"

"I'm okay."

"If you need to talk, I'm always just a phone call away."

"I may take you up on that." Kent let out a long, slow breath, looking her directly in the eye. "By the time I got to the nurses' station, Dr. Franklin was on the floor, and Gretchen started stabbing herself. I lunged toward her, but she plunged the scissors into her neck. Blood went everywhere. I tried to save her."

"I know." Shannon squeezed his biceps. "Nothing more anyone could have done. Any news on Dr. Franklin?"

"Last I heard, he was in surgery, but no one seems very optimistic. It's a bloody mess in there."

"Thanks." In all the years Shannon had been a therapist, she'd only lost three patients to suicide or drug overdose.

But tonight, she'd lost one to an apparent suicide, and the other...well, she hadn't been given a cause of death yet on Belinda.

The doors to the unit opened. Two policemen and two men in suits stood at the nurses' station. At the far end of the unit, the hospital morgue placed Gretchen Carson's lifeless body on a gurney. They covered her face with a white, blood-stained sheet.

Erica, the nurse from earlier, talked with one of the men in suits. She had a cut on her face, just under her right eye, and her left arm sported a sling. She pointed to Shannon. The man turned and waved for Shannon to come over.

"I'm detective Rizzoli," he said. "I understand you are the deceased's psychologist."

"Yes. The name is Dr. Shannon Brendel. I've been seeing Gretchen for about a year now."

"We were told you were here earlier this evening. What was Miss Carson's demeanor?"

"She was stable, for the most part. She'd just come off a binge that nearly killed her. Dr. Franklin prescribed some medications to help her come down and stabilize her mood. When I left her, she was still angry, but I didn't consider her a threat to herself or others. Neither did Dr. Franklin."

"Erica, the nurse, mentioned that Miss Carson had

been yelling at Dr. Franklin as she attacked him. Things like how he deserved to die."

"That doesn't sound like my patient. I've never known her to be violent with others," Shannon said. Gretchen had said numerous times that she'd like to see her mother dead, but not once had she ever done anything remotely violent to the person who had caused her incredible agony. So, going after Franklin seemed way out of character.

"The nurse mentioned that Miss Carson also said she was coming after you. Would she have reason to be upset with you?"

"Of course, she did. I'm her therapist. While I provide a safe, non-judgmental environment for my patients, I'm not their friend, and it's my job to call them on their destructive behaviors." Shannon stuffed her hands deep into her pockets. She hadn't meant to sound defensive. The detective was just doing his job.

Covering all his bases.

Even if that meant pushing her buttons.

"So, is it safe to assume you were who she was angry with when you left? You did say she was angry," the detective said.

"She deflected her anger on me, which is common. However, in my professional opinion, she wasn't in a psychotic state when I left." Shannon couldn't imagine what could have happened to send Gretchen off the deep end. Not even Dr. Franklin's condescending attitude should have been enough to push the young woman into a murdering frenzy.

"Anything else you think we should know?"

Shannon shook her head.

"We're going to need her patient files."

"They are in my office across the street." Shannon pulled out one of her business cards. "I'll need the proper paperwork before I hand them over."

"Not a problem," the detective said. "We'll call before we stop by. Probably early afternoon." The detective walked toward his partner, who was still talking with the morgue personnel.

It was nearly five in the morning, and Shannon wanted to check on Dr. Franklin. She called the desk, and they informed her that he'd survived the surgery but was still in critical condition. They couldn't let her in to see him. While driving home would only take her about twenty minutes or so considering there was no traffic, by the time she got there, she'd only have maybe an hour, then it would be time to head back to the office. There was no point in doing that.

For a brief moment, she thought about canceling her appointments for the day, but the thought of not being busy made her skin crawl. Her patients needed her. And right now, she needed them.

Sitting in the corner of the waiting room, she pulled out her phone and texted Jackson.

Shannon: *I will be at my office all day. Can you send me what you know regarding Belinda?*

Jackson: So far, all I have is they confirmed it's Belinda and are investigating as if it's a murder. That means the police will be tight-lipped. Is everything okay? I'm worried about you.

She wasn't sure if she should be flattered by his sweetness...

Concerned he was getting way too close...

Or both.

Shannon: I had another client die today. So, no, I'm not okay.

Jackson: Shit. Sorry. Where are you?

Shannon: Saratoga Hospital, but headed to my office.

Thank goodness she had a clean set of clothes and a shower thanks to the fact that her office building used to be a home. She couldn't wait to stand under the hot water until it ran winter cold.

Jackson: I'll be by in an hour with some coffee and a breakfast sandwich. I have to do one thing first but hang tight.

Shannon: Okay. Thanks.

Who was she to argue? It wasn't like she needed the man to feel safe. No. It was just because he was working a case that involved her patient.

Besides, she was hungry.

At least, that was the excuse she gave herself.

"Dr. Brendel?" Detective Rizzoli stepped into the waiting room. "Mind if I ask you a couple of additional questions?"

155

"Not at all." She stood, smoothing down her untamed hair.

"Do you agree with the medication the doctor on call prescribed?"

She nodded. "But I'm not a prescribing doctor. It's not my specialty."

"But it's what you would have suggested, correct?"

"Again, I can't make that call. When any of my patients take medication, it's always through a medical doctor. I discuss my therapy findings with the practitioner so they can make an informed decision about my recommendation."

"So, you do make a suggestion, and you play a large role in finding the right dosage."

She nodded, not understanding why any of this was important.

"You and Dr. Franklin don't get along, do you?" the detective asked as he flipped open his notebook.

"We've had our differences, but we always come together to do what's right for the patient." That wasn't a lie. Dr. Franklin might have had an issue with the fact that she was a PhD and not an MD, but he wasn't reckless with patients.

"You had an altercation with him earlier. What was it about?"

"I wouldn't call it that. I generally prefer a non-medication regimen. He's more likely to prescribe, which is always a discussion when it comes to my patients. In this case, the meds were necessary due to

Miss Carson's mental illness and narcotic withdrawal, so I didn't disgaree with him at all. My only issue was in future treatment, which would have been left up to the patient," she said, hoping that would end the questions.

"Let me make sure I have this right. Dr. Franklin wanted to recommend a different strategy regarding therapy? Did he tell you what his plan was? Did he tell the patient?" Rizzoli licked the tip of his pen before pressing it against the notepad.

"He wanted to, but nothing was discussed with me. I don't know about the patient." Shannon blinked. It could be possible that Dr. Franklin had said something to Gretchen that triggered rage, but she'd always been the type to lash out verbally, not physically.

"What about Miss Carson's visitors?"

"I don't know of any visitors other than me," Shannon said.

"The nurse mentioned that a gentleman showed up earlier. Said he didn't stay very long, just dropped something off for you."

"That's impossible," she said, pinching the bridge of her nose. "I didn't send anyone over. Did the nurse get a name?"

"She wasn't given one. Because of the nature of the crime, and the condition of your patient, we'll be requesting an autopsy."

"I think that's a good idea. Do you think something

else happened other than her stabbing the doctor and herself?"

"I honestly don't know what to think. I'll be by your office a little later today with all the proper documentation for Miss Carson's medical records." Rizzoli stuffed his notepad into his coat pocket.

"I'll have them ready." She waited until the detective met up with his partner and sauntered out of the hospital before making a beeline to Kent.

"Hey, doc. Did you forget something?" Kent asked.

"What do you know about a man coming to see my patient?"

Kent rubbed the back of his neck. "I don't know. At least six people came through tonight. I don't know who was here to see whom. They were all to check in at the nurses' station."

"Did anyone stand out as being out of place? Or someone you were concerned about?"

He shook his head. "I tried to give the cops decent descriptions, but we do have people in and out of here all the time. This isn't a locked-down area."

She squeezed his arm. "Not to worry. Call me if you hear anything about Dr. Franklin."

Shannon brushed her bangs out of her face and headed toward the exit. She needed a shower before Jackson came with breakfast.

She also needed a few moments to check the news to see what was being reported about Belinda.

It was going to be a long day, to say the least.

CHAPTER SEVEN

"This has nothing to do with an adoption case."

Jackson punched the gas, pulling out onto the highway, heading south toward Saratoga. It wasn't the worst commute, but he did wonder why the sexy doctor hadn't moved her practice to Lake George since she had decided to live in the village.

Especially when she didn't seem too interested in boating or even being on the water. She'd moved in next door at the beginning of October, so it wasn't like they'd had much time to enjoy water activities, but something told him that her father had ruined sailing for her, and that got under his skin.

Worse, he wanted to know why, and it wasn't because of his profession.

He just wanted to know.

"Her uncle has been sitting at the top of our shared driveway for days. He's tried reaching out to her, and she's blown him off. She doesn't want me to mention her when contacting him, so I figured it's best if you do it."

"What aren't you telling me?" Katie voice screeched through his Bluetooth.

"Everything I don't know."

"Since when don't you speak your suspicions to me?" Katie asked.

"Just call him and follow my script, then tell me what happens. We'll touch base later, and I'll fill you in."

"You're getting personal with this chick, aren't you?"

Jackson had a hard time lying to Katie about anything. Besides having trust issues and hating liars in general, he always told Katie that their partnership had to be based on honesty, even when it was uncomfortable.

"I might be, but I need to respect her privacy on this. She's holding back, and while I suspect the reasons why, I made a promise to her, and I intend to keep it."

"I can live with that."

"Thanks. I appreciate it."

"Hey. I trust you, and if I need to know, you'll tell me," Katie said. "Gotta run. Talk to you later." The phone clicked dead just as he pulled into Shannon's place of work.

It was a renovated house a few blocks from the

hospital. A sign in the front yard had her name on it, as well as the name for a dentist.

That was interesting for a shared business, but whatever worked.

He pulled into a spot next to her vehicle, snagged the bag of bagels and coffee, and made his way to the entrance. He didn't know if he should knock or just walk in. He stood and stared at the door for a long moment before twisting the knob and letting himself into a nice but scantly decorated waiting area.

She had a couch on the north wall and two chairs on the south side with a table between them. But the door to what he believed was her office held a stand with a coffee pot.

He knocked three times, noting the impressive paintings. The woman had good taste—or her decorator did.

"Door's open," Shannon called.

"I brought food." He stepped into her office, holding up the bag and a fresh mug of bitter brew.

"You are the best." She stepped from behind her desk, tucking damp hair behind her ears and adjusting her bangs.

He set everything down and rested his hands on her hips. He knew she shouldn't, but he couldn't resist the pull she had over him. Or the desire. "How are you holding up?"

"Not well, honestly." She placed her hands on his

shoulders. "I can't thank you enough for bringing me food. You didn't have to drive all this way."

"I wanted to see you."

"To talk about Be—"

He pressed his mouth against her plump lips. She tasted like wintergreen on a cool summer's night. He pulled her closer, feeling her full breasts against his chest.

Shannon was different than his ex-wife, Jasmine. Besides not being independently wealthy, Shannon had heart. She cared deeply about those around her, even if she obviously had some serious daddy issues. He'd told himself when he left Jasmine that he wouldn't get involved with another woman who had issues with men.

Except here he was, in a lip-lock with a lady he didn't know or understand, and yet he felt like he'd known her forever.

He took a step back. "I did—I *do* want to talk to you about your client, but I also wanted to see you and make sure you were okay."

"I will be, and food and more caffeine will certainly help." She snagged a bagel and hopped up onto the corner of her desk. "I spoke to your friend, Westerfield."

"He's a good cop."

"He seems to think Belinda was murdered and that her new boyfriend, Clayton, who is now missing, did it."

"They think he's at the bottom of the lake."

Shannon took a big bite of her bagel and nodded. "Murder-suicide?"

"Is that what Westefield told you?" Jackson asked.

"He was tight-lipped about a lot of things," Shannon admitted. "I asked them about her roommate, Janice, as well, but they refused to comment."

"My partner, Katie, and I are going to pay her a visit later today." The only reason he was going to follow up was because of Shannon. Otherwise, there was no reason. His case was over. "Whatever I find out, I'll pass on to you."

"I appreciate that." She swung her legs back and forth. "I've lost patients before, though not many. But two in twenty-four hours…it's too much."

"Do you want to talk about it?" He grabbed his coffee and made himself comfortable on the sofa, glancing around. She displayed nothing personal, and yet she managed to make the space feel homey and comfortable.

"Not much to say. My patient relapsed and then had a bad reaction to withdrawal or managed to get drugs while in the hospital. She ended up killing herself and harming others."

Jackson pulled off the top of the paper mug and set it aside. He blew into the dark liquid. "There's something Westerfield probably didn't tell you."

"What's that?"

"There's no way it was murder-suicide with Belinda

because he believes the body was moved to Long Island."

"Then why did he tell me that?"

Jackson shrugged. "Knowing Westerfield, he was probably trying to gain more insight, or he's making sure the press and the public don't have the details because he's sure the killer is still out there, watching and waiting."

Shannon set her bagel down and wiped her mouth. "I can't imagine who would want to kill Belinda."

"She had a past, and it wasn't pleasant. And from what Westerfield told me, the new boyfriend wasn't much better. He was involved in some underground sex club and—"

Shannon knocked her coffee to the floor. "Fuck."

Jackson quickly set his cup on the table and snagged a few napkins, racing to clean up the mess. "In the six months or so I've known you, I don't think I've ever heard you say that word."

"There is a time and place for everything, and that was some damn good coffee."

"You can finish mine."

"Don't mind if I do." She jumped from the desk, just as Jackson's cell rang out.

She stumbled forward. Her arms flapped wildly, and she landed right on top of him, shoving him onto his back.

"We really have to stop meeting like this." He wrapped his arms around her and planted a quick kiss on her rosy lips before helping her to her feet and finding his phone. "It's my partner, I need to answer it." He tapped the green button. "Hello."

"I spoke to your girlfriend's uncle."

Jackson's heart fluttered.

"And?" He turned as his cheeks flushed. He faced the bookshelf and folded his arm across his middle.

"Well, he didn't have a good relationship with his brother the last few years before Dwight died, but he recently moved back to town, and he's trying to reconnect with family."

"Are you buying that?"

"Yes, and no," Katie said.

"Why?"

"Because he moved from Vermont to Lake George, so really not a big move, and the only reaching out he's done has been to Shannon via sitting at the top of your driveway and a few phone calls. But I did find out that he was busted when he was in his thirties. Something about giving some dude a blowjob in the parking lot of a park."

"That's interesting." Jackson glanced over his shoulder. Shannon sat on the sofa with her feet tucked up under her butt as she pulled at the last few bites of her raisin cinnamon bagel. "How is this important?"

"I take it you're not alone."

"Correct."

"Well, to my knowledge, he's not gay. Or at least he's not out of the closet. He's divorced with a couple of kids and currently in a relationship with a chick he works with."

"What else do I need to know?"

"After I talked to him, I took it upon myself to do a little research, and the arresting officer was someone Jacob knows, so I gave him a call. It turns out that arrest was the reason Ned and his brother Dwight had a falling out."

"Interesting. Why?"

"Jacob's friend, now retired, stated that Dwight let his brother spend the weekend in jail. When he picked him up, he made a comment about getting caught, and Ned's response was something to the effect of being out. That he was done, and he never wanted to see Dwight again. Dwight mentioned that could be arranged."

"Even more interesting."

"I'm not done yet."

Jackson held up his hand and stepped into the waiting room. "I'm listening." He rolled his neck.

"Jacob's buddy, actually more like a friend of his dad's, Jeromy Rimes, was working on some sort of sex club ring back in the day. Guess who was on the long list of suspects."

"Shit. Both of them?"

"Neither was until this incident, but they were more concerned about underage sex trafficking intel that was coming their way. They tailed Ned and Dwight for a good couple of months and found nothing."

"Did they ever close that sex ring?"

"Not really," Katie said. "They've busted different married men parties that have orgies. It's an ongoing battle. They focus on the ones that deal in underage girls and boys and often ignore swingers and such."

"Makes sense." Jackson paced in the waiting room, rubbing his temple as a picture formed in his brain. "What kind of similarities are there between what Clayton was involved in and what Shannon's uncle was?" he asked as quietly as possible.

"I didn't do much poking around on that. Yet. I take it you want me to keep working this, even though it has nothing to do with our little adoption case."

"Actually, I think it does."

"That's a bold statement. Care to elaborate?"

"It's pretty complicated," Jackson said. "For now, can you start a file on Shannon's father and start digging?"

"Truth be told, I already did."

"Thanks."

"My pleasure. I'll touch base with you in a couple of hours."

He tucked his cell into his back pocket and stepped back into Shannon's office.

She'd sprawled out on the sofa with her forearm over her eyes.

He sat on the edge of the couch, resting his hand on her thigh.

She twitched, peeking an eye out from behind her elbow. "What did Katie have to say?"

This was going to be harsh, and he wasn't sure she was ready for him to go down this road, but it was time. "We need to talk, and it's not going to be easy."

She bolted to a sitting position. "I've got a client coming in less than an hour, and I still have to deal with the fallout from two dead patients."

He palmed her cheek and searched her light blue orbs for all answers to the dark questions that had been slowly forming in his mind for the last couple of days. His birth mother's story had been typical. Nothing out of the ordinary. A teenage girl in trouble and she waited too long, so the choice was taken out of her hands. She tried to take care of him but being a drug addict compounded the issue. When things got too tough, she left him.

His five sisters all had similar stories, except for the youngest.

Her birth mother had been raped by her step-brother. When his sister found out about the circumstances of her existence, it had messed with her head.

To be the product of rape could fuck with a kid in ways that no therapist could turn around.

"We can do this later, if you like. But it's important." He shifted, facing her dead-on. "I don't want to stress you out more because I get you've got a lot on your plate right now, but I think it's important we start this conversation as soon as possible."

"Is it about my daughter?"

Fuck. This was going to be harder than he'd thought. "I don't have any more information about her yet. However, I'm forming some connections that I don't like."

"And what's that?" She folded her arms across her chest and tilted her head, completely closing herself off.

He shouldn't be surprised. She was one of the strongest people he'd ever met. But shutting down emotions often took the toughest and shattered them into tiny little pieces.

"There are a lot of things about Belinda and Clayton's murders, and what Clayton was involved in, and what a retired cop believes your uncle Ned and maybe your father were—"

"Stop talking." She stood, smoothing her hands down her slacks.

"I don't mean to be disrespectful, and I don't want to cause you any pain."

She nodded. "My mother just pulled in." She pointed toward the open door that led to the waiting room. "Whatever you're uncovering, don't ever go to my mother or my sisters with any of it."

———

"What the hell do you think you're doing?"

"Nice to see you, too, mother," Shannon said, letting

out a long breath. Her mind spun with everything that Jackson had tossed at her in a matter of seconds.

Not to mention her patients.

"I'm going to get going." Jackson squeezed her forearm. "I'll see you tonight."

Her mother folded her arms and tapped her open-toed shoe. "I didn't realize someone was here." She looked Jackson up and down. "I'm surprised you're one of my daughter's patients."

"I'm not," Jackson said. "Although, if I was in need of a good therapist, I'd choose Shannon." He smiled that sweet, kind smile of his that made her go all weak in the knees and made her want to forget who she was and where she'd come from.

"Perhaps you had a hand in what happened last night with Tara." Her mother glared with condemnation in her eyes.

"Is something wrong with my sister?" Shannon clutched her pendant. "What happened? Is she okay? Where is she?"

"Vegas. With Kevin," her mother said with disdain. "She's ruining Bonnie's wedding. You should have seen poor Bonnie this morning when she found out that your little sister ran off to get married. And in Vegas of all places." Her mother visibly shivered. "They didn't name that place Sin City for no reason."

Jackson mouthed, *"I need to go."* He leaned in and kissed Shannon's cheek. "I'm really sorry, but I have an appointment, and this is family business. It was good to see you again, Melinda."

Before Shannon could even bat an eyelash, Jackson was out the door and climbing into his big, honking pickup.

Shannon closed her eyes, sucked in a deep breath, and counted to ten.

"I hate it when you do that. It's as if you're ignoring me," her mother said under her breath.

"Because I am." Shannon blinked, letting the air out of her lungs. "So, Tara and Kevin eloped?" The corners of her mouth tugged upward. She couldn't be happier —or prouder—of her little sister for finally standing up for what she wanted. "Good for them."

"Did you put that little idea in her head?" Her mother tossed her purse onto the chair and slapped her hands on her thighs. "Not only is she upstaging Bonnie's upcoming nuptials, but Kevin left a note telling his father that he quit the firm. Can you believe that? He just up and quit a perfectly good job."

"Did you ever think maybe he has a better one lined up?"

Her mother stomped her foot and planted her hands on her hips. "So, you *did* know? And you probably made their travel arrangements. I should have known you'd sabotage my plans."

"You're the one who wanted them back together." Why Shannon even chose to engage her mother at this point was beyond her, especially with the day she'd had and what was on the horizon.

Maybe it was a good distraction.

"Of course, I do. Kevin and Tara are a power couple."

"Jesus, Mother. Do you hear yourself?"

"Don't use God's name in vain."

Shannon laughed. As if her mother really believed in God. She used religion as a way to cleanse her soul. To keep her good standing in the community. Part of Shannon wished she could find comfort in the arms of the church, but all it did was remind her of the hypocrisy of her entire childhood. "Can't you just be happy for Tara and Kevin? This is what they want. It might not be how *you* wanted it to happen, but can't you see how your meddling might have pushed them into it?"

"Seriously? You're going to blame me for this when I trusted you with Tara? I dropped her off there so you could help her and Kevin see their future, not push them away." Her mother dabbed her eyes. "Now, they are going to move to Newburgh. Who the hell lives in that godawful place?"

Wonderful. *Here comes the waterworks.*

"Mom. It's going to be okay. They will only be a few hours away, and it's not going to upstage Bonnie's wedding." Nothing could ever take center stage from that woman.

"You're not a mother. You don't understand."

Shannon gasped, clutching her gut. Never in her life had she considered herself a mom.

But she *had* given birth to a little girl.

"Oh, stop," her mother chided. "We are not going down *that* road." She tilted her chin. "Now, I expect you to get ahold of Tara and tell her to get her ass back here. And if she and Kevin managed to get married last night, then tell them they'd better get it annulled and not breathe a word of it. We can plan a big wedding for them next year."

"Mom, they don't want that. Do you ever listen to anything your children want or don't want?"

"That's no way to speak to your mother." She fanned her face. "Why do you always do this to me? What did I do to deserve this?"

There was no reasoning with her mother, and it was pointless to continue the conversation. Besides, Lilly's father and his wife should be in her office in the next ten minutes. The last thing she needed was her mother, the train wreck, there when Lilly and her father and stepmother showed up.

"I'll call Tara."

"Thank you," her mother said. "I'm glad you've come to your senses."

Shannon bit down on the inside of her cheek. She had no intention of trying to talk Tara into coming home, but she *would* congratulate her, that was for damn sure.

"I'd better run. I'll see you later in the week." Her

mother grabbed her purse, turned on her heel, and strolled out the door like she was the Queen of England.

Talk about exhausting.

Shannon rubbed the back of her neck and glanced at her phone, smiling. Jackson had sent her a text.

Jackson: If you need me, I'm just a phone call away. See you tonight.

She didn't have a chance to respond or even gather her thoughts before Greg and his lovely but distraught wife came barreling through her door.

"Good morning," Shannon said. "Where's Lilly?"

"She's not coming." Greg wrapped his arm around his wife, Julie. "She left home."

"What do you mean?" Shannon couldn't handle another patient with issues. Of course, all her clients had problems. That's why they came to see a therapist in the first place. Although Shannon thought everyone should see one at some point in their life.

"She snuck out last night and left this note." Julie handed a crumpled piece of paper to Shannon. "She was doing so well, and then her mother showed up out of the blue, and everything changed."

"When did her mother get out of rehab?" Shannon held the note and made her way to the filing cabinet, pulling out Lilly's file.

"Two days ago. But not because she was done with treatment." Greg ran a hand over his unshaven face. "Sally was doing so well. The last time I spoke to her, she was excited about the way things were going for Lilly, and she seemed truly happy for Lilly's fresh start. If Sally is back to using and back to her old ways, this won't be good for our daughter."

"Lilly is strong, and she's made more progress than you realize." Shannon set the file on the top of her desk and unfolded the piece of paper that Lilly had left her parents.

Dear Dad and Julie,

Thanks. I just can't live here or like this. I'm too broken. I appreciate all you've done, but my mom needs me. And, truthfully, I need her.

Lilly.

Shannon glanced up. "Lilly didn't write this."

"Excuse me?" Greg blinked. "That's her handwriting. We double-checked it against her schoolbooks."

"That very well may be true, but it's the language. This isn't her voice. It's not how she would have chosen to tell you." Shannon flipped open the file. "Not only are the words wrong, but she would have doodled over her signature. It's her thing. Look."

Greg glanced between the papers on the desk and Shannon. "I don't understand."

"When was the last time you spoke with Lilly?" Shannon asked as she lifted the phone.

"Yesterday, before she went to bed. We had all gone out for ice cream. We actually had a wonderful night."

Shannon let out a long breath. "Have you called the police?"

Greg nodded. "They took a report, but they don't consider her missing—"

"I know the drill. But do you mind if I call a friend who specializes in finding people?"

"Doc, you're scaring us." Julie swiped at her eyes. "We just thought something happened to her mother in rehab to set her back and that she went AWOL and came after Lilly. And you know the effect Sally has on her daughter when Sally's deep in her addiction."

"I do. And it's a cycle that's hard to break," Shannon said.

"Do you think her mother has her?" Greg asked.

"That's the likely scenario. With your permission, I'd like to ask my friend to go to all of Sally's old stomping grounds to find them."

"We can't afford—"

"Let me worry about that for now." Shannon had no idea how she would pay Jackson for this one, but she couldn't let another patient down.

Not today.

She brought up his contact information. It rang twice.

"So, you missed me already," Jackson said with a touch of sweetness.

"How far away are you?"

"I'm actually still in Saratoga. I had some business here," Jackson said. "Are you okay?"

"Not really. Can you come back to my office? I have an underage patient who appears to have run away.

Her father and stepmother are in my office. They've called the police, but she's done this before, and they won't do anything until it's been twenty-four hours."

"I'm on my way. Give me ten minutes."

"Thanks." She set the handle in the cradle. "My friend, Jackson, will be here shortly. For now, why don't you get a cup of coffee and make yourselves comfortable? I'm going to call the rehab center where Sally was staying and see what I can find out."

"Do you always go this far for your patients?" Greg asked.

"No," she admitted. "But I don't believe Lilly left that note, and I'm not about to wait for the cops to decide she's in trouble."

CHAPTER EIGHT

Jackson didn't like checking up on the girl he currently wanted to date. It felt like a total invasion of privacy. He tried to convince himself it was about her adoption case.

But it wasn't.

"Thanks for meeting with me," Jackson said, sticking out his hand as he made himself comfortable on the park bench outside the village.

"My pleasure." Jeromy Rimes couldn't be older than sixty-five, but he wore his age like a badge of honor with his deep-set lines around his eyes, and his gray brows. He wasn't a tall man at five-foot-eight, but he was broad.

And muscular.

A well-built machine, even at his age.

"I hear you work with Katie. How's that going?"

"Interesting," Jackson admitted.

"I bet. Her personality matches her fiery red hair. But deep down, she's a sweet girl who's been handed a raw deal."

"Agreed." Jackson glanced around. It was getting dark, and he had a million things to do, but he had to meet with Jeromy—for more than one reason. "I don't have much time, so I hope you don't mind if I cut to the chase."

"Not at all."

"What can you tell me about Ned Brendel and the sex club ring case you were working?"

Jeromy arched a brow. "Wow. That's a name I haven't heard in a long time, though I just saw him a few hours ago."

"Really? Where?"

"I had lunch with him."

That wasn't something Jackson had expected. "You're friends?" He shifted, taking his cowboy hat off and setting it on the bench.

"I wouldn't go that far. But ever since I arrested him, humiliated him, and ruined his marriage, we've kept in touch," Jeromy said with a slight chuckle, shaking his head.

Jackson rubbed his jaw. He couldn't tell if Jeromy meant his response to be flippant, tongue and cheek, or on point. "You made nine arrests after Ned, all related to men having sex with underage girls and boys."

Jeromy nodded. "No thanks to Ned."

"I'm sorry. But I'm not following any of this."

"Let's backtrack this," Jeromy said. "Before I busted Ned, a teenage girl came to me and told me her stepfather had *sold* her into a sex club where his friends passed her around."

"Jesus," Jackson mumbled.

"It was fucking gross." Jeromy raked a hand through his hair. "She had the name of one man, other than her stepfather, and that was Ned Brendel. So, we put a tail on him. I might have jumped the gun when I busted him in the park because I never got any names from him. But he did give me some information on where some of the club meetings were held."

"That's how you made your arrests?"

Jeromy nodded. "But no one would ever give anyone up, and this bullshit is still going on, as you know from this latest murder."

"I don't know that much. Westerfield isn't giving me a ton of intel at this point."

"Well, I'm a private citizen these days. What do you need to know to help you with whatever case you're working on?"

What a fucking loaded question that was? And Jackson wasn't even sure if he was asking to help find Lilly...

Or Shannon's daughter at this point.

He might as well pull out all the stops.

"Do you think Ned's brother was involved in this sex club?"

Jeromy arched a brow. "Before I answer that, why do you want to know?"

"I can't tell you."

"Fair enough," Jeromy said. "I know for a fact that Dwight Brendel was one of the leaders. I just could never prove it. But he's dead. So, what are you going to do?"

"Where did they get the girls?"

"That's truly the sad part."

Jackson held his breath as his heart sank to his gut like a cement brick. "This wasn't human trafficking, was it?"

"Nope. Nothing worse than adults taking full advantage of young girls and boys and abusing their trust."

"Fuck," Jackson muttered. His thoughts had gone into a very dark place, and Shannon was at the center of it.

Jeromy leaned forward. "Belinda was a victim of that sex club. Her father used to sell her to the highest bidder during his Tuesday poker games. They'd take turns while he dealt."

"That's really fucked up." Jackson couldn't suck in a deep breath if he tried. A wave of nausea gripped him so tight, he thought he might pass out if he tried to stand. "How do you know all this?"

"I arrested Belinda's father ten years ago when she was only fourteen years old."

Jackson leaned back on the bench and stared across

the street at the lake, just as a sailboat caught wind and cut through the water.

No one had such dark rituals with that much hatred for their father unless they had a really good reason.

"Did you know Belinda?" Jackson asked.

"Not well. But I heard she was seeing a therapist." Jeromy cocked his head. "Shannon Brendel."

A sharp pain stabbed Jackson in the center of his chest and ripped through his entire body.

"She's a sharp girl, and I hear she's really good at what she does. But I can see you've gone to the same place I've been living for years, and I'm going to take you to an even darker place."

"I'm not sure I can handle that." But Jackson wasn't going to stop the man.

"Have you ever met her stepmother, Annette?"

Jackson shook his head. "Just her mother, Melinda."

"She's a piece of work. Fucking bitch turned a blind eye to the whole thing and still pretends it never happened."

Jackson swallowed.

"But Annette, she's something else. And she did something about it."

"Did what?"

"This is where it gets really dicey, and I don't know the whole story, but I've always suspected that Dwight was one of the leaders in the sex club ring, and that Shannon was a victim. She disappeared from—"

"What do you mean, disappeared?"

"She went to *rehab.*" Jerome used his fingers to make air quotes. "But I was never able to verify that.

The baby.

"I wanted to put a tail on Dwight, but my captain wouldn't let me. By that time, a few years had passed, other sex crimes had come and gone, and no more girls had come forward."

Jackson balled his fists. "Did anyone talk to Shannon?"

"She was a minor. We couldn't. Not without her parents present. We approached her mother, and that didn't go over well. But Annette, she was a different story, though she wasn't a parent or a guardian."

"How long were Annette and Shannon's father married?"

"Less than three years," Jeromy said. "Thing is, we busted an orgy at the motel up by Hoisers Bar two weeks before Dwight died. One young man by the name of Alex Angler worked for Dwight. That was enough for my captain to give me the thumbs-up to at least have a conversation. When I got nowhere with the mother, I went to Annette. I was disappointed that she defended her husband so vehemently, but I could tell she was totally disgusted by what I told her."

"Do you think she knew what was going on?"

Jeromy shook his head. "No. Actually, I think the poor woman was shocked. A week later, the man was dead."

"Are you accusing Annette of killing him?"

Jeromy shook his head. "No. The man died of a heart attack. But I question her story."

"Could you please just be direct?"

"She told the first responders that she went to bed before her husband and woke up to find him dead. But she told me that he was asleep when she came to bed but had been complaining of heartburn."

"That sounds like you believe Annette had a hand in his death."

"What I believe is that Dwight was a monster, and while Ned wouldn't tell me shit eighteen years ago or even ten years ago, he's since had a change of heart and has been slowly giving me some information, in a weird way. The players have changed, but not how the club works."

Jackson pinched the bridge of his nose. "I live next to Shannon, and for the last few days, I've seen Ned's car at the top of my driveway. Why?"

"You'd have to ask him that."

"I'm asking you."

"Best guess is he's concerned, considering the sex clubs have been popping up left and right lately." Jeromy stood. "Perhaps it's time you have a long, serious chat with Shannon."

Jackson planned on doing exactly that. But first, he had to try to find Lilly. His cell vibrated in his back pocket. He pulled it out and glanced at the screen.

Katie.

"Hey, partner, what's up?" He meandered toward his pickup.

"I've got some interesting news."

"Lay it on me." He pointed his key fob toward his vehicle. It beeped twice, igniting Jackson's headache.

"First, I just scanned and emailed some information that came over from the adoption agency in Rochester where Shannon gave birth."

"And?"

"I didn't read it all, but we found her daughter."

Jackson tossed his cowboy hat across the cab of his truck. He'd need to rifle through that file before telling Shannon anything. "What else?"

"You might want to hold onto your hat for this one. Janice, Belinda's roommate, well, she was involved in the sex ring."

"Excuse me? Isn't that mainly men with sex addictions who like young girls, and in some cases boys?"

"That's one aspect, but it seems this particular ring is filled with all sorts of surprises. And I have a name of a man that Janice says is at the center of it."

"You talked to Janice?"

"She was arrested an hour ago," Katie said. "She and a few friends were at a hotel having a party, and at the center of that little gathering was a young boy performing sex acts with adults."

"That's gross."

"I know, but she gave up the name of the man who

brought her in and sets everything up. His name is Alex Angler."

"What do you know about him?"

"Not much. I'll work on it tonight and send you an email as soon as I have something."

"I appreciate it. I'll check in later." He climbed behind the steering wheel and contemplated calling Shannon, but what would he say? He'd wait until he had more or until he saw her in person.

Jackson spent half the night combing the streets for a drug addict and her kid and found nothing but reminders of why he shouldn't be looking for Shannon's daughter. It didn't matter that he knew that Shannon's motivations were pure. She wouldn't intentionally harm her daughter, but just coming into her kid's life could cause a ripple effect of emotions that couldn't be stopped.

However, no matter how hard he tried, he couldn't shake the idea that what had happened to Belinda and her new boyfriend and their crazy, weird sex ring was somehow related to Shannon's uncle.

And maybe the reason Shannon had given up her daughter.

Or had gotten pregnant in the first place.

Not to mention, Shannon's father and the cold,

harsh words that Jeromy had spoken about Dwight Brendel.

Jackson swallowed the bile that smacked the back of his throat as he pulled into the shared driveway and his parking spot next to Shannon's SUV. The sun peeked out over the mountains, turning the night sky into morning. He slipped from behind the steering wheel, surprised to see Shannon standing on the dock in front of *Sweet Freedom.*

Stuffing his keys into his pocket, he adjusted his cowboy hat and made his way down the path. If he'd gotten an hour's worth of sleep, it would have been a miracle. He would need to rest his eyes for a few hours at some point, but for now, he needed to have this chat with Shannon. He hoped he had the energy for it, because it wasn't going to be pretty.

She glanced over her shoulder as his feet hit the wooden planks.

"Did you get any sleep? You look like hell."

"Gee, thanks," he said with a smile. "I might have dozed off for a few minutes here or there in my car."

"Now I feel terrible for asking you to go looking for Lilly."

"Don't. I'm happy to help." He ran a hand up and down her forearm. "We have a lot to talk about, and I don't want to do it standing on this dock." He tilted his head toward the aft of his boat.

Her eyes went wide, and she shook her head.

"Why not? It's just a sailboat. It doesn't bite."

"Actually, it does." She plopped herself onto the dock and dangled her feet in the water.

"Do you want to tell me what happened that makes you so afraid of sailboats?" he asked.

"I'm not afraid of them. It's just not something I enjoy."

"I'm not asking you to go sailing. Just to have a seat on the stern where it's more comfortable." Jackson rubbed his chin, and his mind continued to form a picture that soured his belly and squeezed his heart.

"I'm comfortable right here," she said. "I take it you didn't find Lilly."

"No sign of her or her mother anywhere. Not a single one of her mother's old friends has heard from her."

"That's disturbing," Shannon said. "That's usually the first place addicts go, even with a kid in tow."

"I know." Jackson kicked off his boots, tugged off his socks, rolled up his jeans, and joined her on the dock, wishing he could talk her into his plush stern sofa. But he wouldn't push that today. Not when he was about to poke a different bear, and especially not before he told her he'd found her daughter. "Katie is still pounding the pavement."

"I feel like I'm using you and your business partner."

He looped his arm around her waist. "We're invested in this case in more ways than one."

"What does that mean?"

"There are a lot of moving parts that don't seem to

be connected but are." He had no idea how to approach the subject. He suspected that she'd dealt with the pains of her childhood, considering she was a therapist who specialized in addiction, though her ritual and her inability to board his boat spoke volumes. "For example, your uncle Ned and what he was involved in when he was arrested. And your client, Belinda, and what she, her new boyfriend, and her roommate were doing with some guy by the name of Alex Angler."

———

"Alex Angler?" The name scorched Shannon's throat as she barely managed to say the words. She tried to swallow, but her muscles wouldn't work.

A slight breeze kicked up, rattling the sail against the mast of Jackson's sailboat.

A guttural sob filled her gut. She gasped.

"Are you all right?" Jackson asked.

She sucked in a deep breath, but it didn't fill her lungs. "Are you sure he's involved?" She would have never come back to Lake George if any of those five men still lived in the area. Two of them had retired and moved south. One was dead. And that left Alex and Borden. She believed that Borden lived in San Diego now and was told that Alex had a career in New York City. She worried that he might vacation up here or visit, but she hadn't seen him since the day she'd buried her father.

"You know him?"

"Don't answer a question with a question." Tears stung her eyes. Her body shook from the inside out. When she decided to find her little girl, she'd stirred up a lot of emotional baggage, and that had brought back the night that she knew—without a doubt—that her daughter had been conceived. She glanced over her shoulder and stared at the stupid Tartan. Damn fucking gorgeous sailboat. If she were any other woman, she'd give her right arm to go for a ride on the stupid thing.

"Based on my intel, I'm sure he's the ringleader," Jackson said. "How do you know him?"

"He knew my father," Shannon admitted, clutching her pendant. She ran her finger up and down the feather. When she'd first met Alex, he was a nineteen-year-old kid working at her father's office for the summer. She'd just turned fourteen.

A year later, she was stuck in the bow of her father's boat while Alex and a few of her father's so-called friends took turns with her while dear old Dad sat behind the helm, drinking his beer and soaking in the sun. She actually didn't know what he did or thought. By the time he made his way to the galley, he was drunk, and she was curled up in a ball in a corner.

At first, Alex had been sort of sweet and gentle. It was as if he wasn't sure what he was doing or why, and the first time she'd ever done a line of cocaine had been with him. He'd taught her how to numb the pain. For a short time, he'd been sort of a friend.

Until he changed.

And not for the better.

"I take it you knew him, as well?" Jackson looped his arm around her waist, giving her a gentle squeeze.

She stiffened.

He dropped his hand.

But she couldn't relax.

"Shannon. I don't like asking you to talk about things that upset you. However, your patient's murder appears to be connected to this man. With your uncle's history and him showing up, my mind is forming a pretty ugly picture of what happened to you."

"I can't do this." Her heart raced.

"You're going to have to. The police will be questioning you about what you know, especially since a couple of your patients are involved."

This couldn't be happening. Her past couldn't be colliding with her present. Her mother had always told her it was best to keep skeletons locked up in the closet, never letting them out.

Could she have let out her worst nightmare by starting the search for her kid?

She jumped up but lost her footing. Her arms flapped wildly as she tried to regain her balance.

Jackson reached for her, but it was too late as she splashed into the icy waters of Lake George.

Her body jerked. She kicked and scrambled for the

surface. As soon as her head lifted out of the water, she gasped for air. "Holy mother of God, that's fucking cold."

Jackson leaned over and heaved her out of the water. He lifted her into his arms and jogged down the dock.

"Put me down," she said.

"When I get you inside and wrapped in a towel." He adjusted her in his arms. "I'll put on a pot of coffee, make you some breakfast, and we'll—"

"I can't."

He kissed her cheek before bending over and opening her back door.

"You don't understand."

He set her down by the bathroom door and found a towel, handing it to her. "Try me."

"You'll just judge me for not doing anything."

"You were a child," he said with a dark tone. "Why don't you go get some dry clothes on, and I'll make you something to eat? When do you have to leave for the office?"

"I don't. I canceled all my appointments today, and I'll be doing paperwork from home. One of the detectives will be stopping by around lunch." Flashes of her childhood filled her mind. The fear that tore through her soul with the first contraction tugged at her heart. The sound of her little girl crying filled her ears.

That child was innocent.

She hadn't asked to be born from violence.

But she deserved a chance at a good life, and Shannon wanted to give her that.

Jackson held her chin between his thumb and forefinger. "Let me in, Shannon. I'm on your side. Telling me what you know, what happened to you, before you have to explain any of it to the police will only make it easier."

Breathe. Just breathe. "Okay. Give me five minutes." She turned and raced up the stairs, tears streaming down her face. She stepped into her bedroom and took her cell from its cradle on the nightstand. She found Annette's contact information and hit send.

"Hi, dear, what's going on?"

Shannon sobbed.

"Honey, what's the matter?"

"Alex Angler is back."

Silence on the other end.

"Did you hear me?"

"I did," Annette said. "How do you know?"

"He's heading up a sex ring that my clients are involved in. *My patients*, Annette. Mine. Don't you think that's a little convenient?" She sniffled. "Do you remember what he said to me at Dad's funeral?" She shivered. Alex had had the audacity to wrap his arms around her, pull her close, and whisper in her ear, *"Someday, I'll return for what is rightfully mine."*

Did he actually believe Shannon belonged to him?

"I do," Annette said calmly. "Honey. Where are you?"

193

"At home."

"Are you alone?"

"Jackson's here." Shannon set the phone to speaker and towel-dried her hair as she slipped out of her wet clothes. "He's the one who told me."

"I'm glad you're not alone. I take it you've told him everything?"

"No. But he's pieced most of it together, and I'm going to have to tell the police what I know." Shannon stood in front of her mirror in her bra and panties and pressed her hand over her stomach, fingering her stretch marks. The one thing she could never truly hide. Of course, she always wore one-piece bathing suits, and she'd told the few men who questioned her about it that she used to be fat as a kid.

"You've kept this locked up inside you for so long. And I get why, but—"

"I know I have to." Standing there staring at herself, a grown woman who'd survived some of the worst trauma a child could ever have to endure, she realized she'd done it. She'd made something of herself, and she'd be damned if she would let her past—*Alex*—ruin everything she'd worked so hard for.

"Would you like me to drive up tonight?" Annette asked.

"Do you mind putting that on the back burner for now? I'll call you this afternoon."

"I'll clear my schedule for the rest of the weekend. Hubby will understand."

"Thanks, Annette. I love you."

"I love you, too."

Shannon let out a long breath, tapped the red circle on her cell, turned, and gasped. Wrapping her hands around her middle, she stared at Jackson, holding two mugs.

"Oh, shit. I'm sorry." He turned. "I just thought you might like some coffee."

"I do." She snagged an oversized T-shirt and pulled it over her head, then hiked up a pair of sweatpants. "I'm decent." She plopped herself onto the bed and took the cup he offered. "I owe you an apology for how I just reacted."

"No. You don't." He leaned against the window and brought the coffee to his lips and blew.

"When I asked you to find my little girl, I never expected what the next few days would bring up."

"You have a great view of my sailboat." Jackson opened the curtains. "I have a lot of things swirling around in my brain and..." He let his words trail off while he ran a hand over his face. "My youngest sister is the only one of us that has a relationship with her birth mother."

"What does—"

He held up his hand. "All of us had questions about where we came from—at least the biology. But Jeanie, my youngest sister, when she went looking for her birth parents, she had just turned eighteen. All my other sisters had relatively positive experiences, and my birth mother hadn't come gunning for me yet."

"You make it sound like your mother was a predator."

"She was." Jackson took another long sip of his coffee. "But you're not, and neither is Hannah."

"Who is Hannah?"

"Jeanie's birth mother."

"Why are we talking about this?" Not that Shannon didn't appreciate the reprieve from her problems. It gave her strength to form the words she hadn't spoken outside of therapy in years.

"Just let me finish." He caught her gaze. His dark eyes captivated her in a way made her feel cared for and understood.

The only person who'd ever looked at her that way was Annette.

Shannon nodded.

"Jeanie was born with a congential disability, and she always thought that's why her parents gave her up. She wanted them to tell her she was glad they had. That she had a wonderful life with a great family."

Shannon let the tears flow. "That's all I want for my baby."

Jackson nodded. "So, it came as quite a surprise when Jeanie found out that her mother hadn't even known she had been born with problems and that Hannah had only been fourteen when she gave birth."

"Oh, no." Shannon set her coffee on her nightstand

and inched across the room. "Hannah was raped, wasn't she?"

"By her stepbrother. For a long time, that messed with my sister's head."

Shannon placed her hand on Jackson's shoulder. "I hope Jeanie understands that how she came to be has nothing to do with who she is."

"It took a good therapist—one like you—for her to figure that out." He kissed her temple. "I don't need to know the dirty details, but I hurt for what your father did to you. If he were still alive, I'd kill him with my bare hands."

She wrapped her arms around his middle and rested her head on his strong shoulder, staring at *Sweet Freedom*. For him, the boat represented a new chapter in his life. But for her, it was all about everything she wanted to erase from her mind, and yet it held onto the one thing she never wanted to forget.

Her daughter.

No matter how she came into this world, she was a precious gift. Even if she wasn't meant to bring that joy into Shannon's life, she was for someone else.

"The reason I reacted so negatively to your boat was because my daughter was conceived on one just like it."

He reached out and set his coffee on the dresser and hugged her tight.

She'd never felt safer than in his arms.

"It happened right out there on Lake George, up by Paradise Bay. I was sixteen, and my dad liked to bring some of his buddies out and have me act as the galley wench. He thought it was hysterical to call me that."

"It's not funny at all."

She let out a slight laugh. "There were five men that day."

"Jesus. I don't think I want to hear this."

Glancing up at him, she managed a smile. "Alex Angler was one of them, and he could be the father."

"What about the other four?"

"One is dead. The rest don't live anywhere near here and aren't messing with my patients or me."

"And what about Ned?"

"I don't know. I haven't seen or spoken to him in years. My father hated him after he got arrested. I didn't understand it at the time, but I think either Ned embarrassed the group or left. Or both."

"How do you feel about giving him a call and finding out what he wants?" He cupped her cheeks. "I'll put him on speaker and be with you every step of the way."

"Why are you doing this? Whoever hired you to find Belinda, besides me, doesn't need your services anymore."

He brushed her bangs from her eyes, leaning closer, his mouth only an inch from hers. "Isn't it obvious?"

She swallowed her breath before his lips brushed gently across hers in a tender, caring kiss. It wasn't a romantic or sexual kiss.

But it still made her heart race.

"I'm falling for you. Hard."

There was no point in fighting her feelings, which she'd been doing her entire life, but Jackson was special.

She rubbed her fingers across his shoulders, clasping her hands behind his neck. "I'm kind of falling for you, too."

CHAPTER NINE

Jackson leaned against the hood of his truck with his arms folded across his chest. "I don't know how I'm going to tell Shannon this."

"Like you're ripping off a Band-Aid," Katie said. "Are you sure that's her uncle?"

"Positive. And that's Alex Angler."

"They look pretty chummy."

"A little too much." Why the hell would Shannon's uncle be having coffee with Alex? Considering the history and what Jeromy said about Ned, it didn't add up.

Unless Ned was playing both sides of the fence.

The question was…why?

Jackson pulled out his cell and called Jeromy.

"Hey, kid, what's up?"

"Why would Alex and Ned be hanging out together

as if they're old friends?" Jackson often believed in cutting to the chase.

"They wouldn't."

"Except I'm staring at them, and it looks like a friendly conversation."

"That doesn't make sense. Ned has been sort of working with me, like I told you."

"It's the *sort of* that bothers me," Jackson said. "Is there anything else I should know about these two men?"

"They didn't travel in the same circles. Ned was out by the time Alex came into the picture. But if they are talking, maybe Ned is gathering information."

"I don't think so. I better get back to Shannon." He ended the call and tucked his cell into his pocket. The more he learned, the more he realized that Shannon was in grave danger.

———

"I don't know what to say."

Shannon glanced between her long-time friend, Cameron, and Jackson's boat rocking in the breeze. "There's nothing to say." Shannon leaned forward in the chair and took her friend's hand.

"I knew you didn't have a good relationship with your father, but I had no idea."

"Most people didn't," Shannon said. "It's the kind of skeleton you keep buried."

Cameron nodded. "I wouldn't have ever judged you for what you did, you know that, right?"

Shannon smiled. "I do. I've thought about telling you about what happened and about the daughter I gave up a hundred times, but I often didn't believe it was real. I mean, my own mother made me pretend that it never happened, and for a long time, I think I tried to believe that, too."

"God, I'm sorry. But I really don't like your mom."

Shannon opened her mouth, but Cameron held up her hand.

"You make a ton of excuses for her. You always have. Like when she went to your stepsister's graduation over yours. Your mother has not once put you first, and that's not right."

Who was Shannon to argue with that logic? "I know. But she's the only mother I have."

Cameron smiled. "You have Annette. She's stood by you through all of this. I know she's a whackadoodle at times, but she loves you."

"Yeah. She does. And I appreciate her standing by me all these years." Shannon squeezed Cameron's hand. "As I do you. I know I didn't tell you any of this, but I couldn't have gotten through college or my PhD program without you. There is no way I would be the woman I am today, or have the courage to ask Jackson to find my little girl, if it wasn't for you."

Cameron wrapped her arms around Shannon. "You've done the same for me. And no matter what, I'm always in your corner." She leaned back and wiped her cheeks. "You really don't want to meet your little girl?"

"I don't. I let my mother put lies into my head that she didn't exist, and I need to know she's real. That's all."

"I can understand that," Cameron said. "And I support that."

"Thanks. You have no idea what that means to me."

Cameron nodded. "Now. Tell me about Jackson. What's going on there?"

It was impossible not to smile. "I'm not exactly sure, except I really like him. A lot. More than any man I've ever dated."

"So. You're dating now?"

"I wouldn't go that far, but I hope that's where we are headed." Shannon's heart swelled. For the first time in her life, she felt like she might have gotten a taste of what *sweet freedom* might actually feel like.

"Oh, crap." Cameron tapped her Apple watch. "I've got to go. Call me so we can go on a double date."

"Absolutely." Shannon stood, hugging her friend. She watched Cameron slip behind the steering wheel of her vehicle and drive away before stepping into her cottage and putting on a pot of coffee.

She settled at her kitchen table, unable to concentrate on all the paperwork staring her in the face. Her mind kept wandering to Lilly and her mother and worrying about what might have happened to them. She glanced at the clock hanging on the wall.

Three in the afternoon.

Jackson had stepped out. He had some lead on Lilly and her mother and wanted to handle it personally, and Shannon appreciated everything he and his partner were doing to help her with a variety of problems. She just hoped he made it back before her uncle Ned came knocking on her door in half an hour.

Her cell rang, and she jumped.

"Hello?"

"Shannon Brendel?"

"Yes?"

"This is Kent from the hospital."

She pushed her computer to the side. "Hi, Kent. How are you?"

"I'm okay," he said. "I thought I should call to tell you that I saw that guy who visited Gretchen the night she killed herself."

Shannon sat up taller. "You did? Where?"

"He was here talking with some of the staff. He said he was Gretchen's mother's boyfriend, and I overheard him asking about you. I thought you'd want to know."

"Me? Do you have a name?"

"Only a first name. Alex."

Shannon's heart dropped to her gut. "I appreciate you calling me." She ended the call and stared out at *Sweet Freedom*.

When her father died, Alex had felt as though he'd been abandoned by a man who loved him, only Dwight had no feelings for anyone but himself. Alex blamed

Shannon for him losing what he thought was his best friend as well as his connection to the club.

Of course, Shannon had no idea what'd happened to it after her father passed, but she constantly looked over her shoulder for a good year. It wasn't until all the men had left the area that she finally felt safe. Even though she lived a half-hour south, and her mother never brought her to Lake George, that didn't matter. She still worried that she'd run into them or they'd come after her, expecting the same favors her father had promised. And she didn't think she'd be strong enough to say no.

The door rattled, and she gasped. "Shit, you scared me," she said as Jackson stepped into her kitchen.

"You look like you just saw a ghost. What happened?"

She stood, knocking over the chair as she raced into his arms.

"Whoa." He hugged her tightly. "What's going on?"

"It's Alex. He was at the hospital visiting another of my patients." She sobbed into Jackson's shirt. "I tell my patients, all of them, that this isn't their fault and that telling someone is safe. That they can be safe. And yet, because I kept all this a secret, and didn't do anything, that man is out there. And I think he's killing my patients because he blames me for taking my father from him."

"Hey. This is not your fault." Jackson cupped her cheeks. "Even if Alex is coming after you through your patients for whatever sick reason, you still can't hold yourself responsible for his actions."

"But I can hold myself accountable for my inaction." She pounded his chest.

"Did you ever tell anyone?"

She laughed, turning on her heel to pace in her kitchen. "I told my mother once. She called me dramatic and a liar."

"Your mother is a piece of work," Jackson muttered. "Why did they get divorced?"

"Because he couldn't keep his dick in his pants, and he hit her a few times."

"And when you told your mom you were pregnant?"

Shannon opened the front door and took two steps outside. "I told her it was one of my dad's friends, and for about five seconds, she believed me. But then she realized what it might do to her reputation, and she decided that I was high on cocaine—which was true."

"How exactly did your dad die?"

She spun on her heel and gasped. "What did you hear, exactly? And from whom?"

"I know he died of a heart attack, but a retired cop said that Annette's story changed so much, he wasn't sure he believed everything."

Shannon opened her mouth, but Jackson shushed her with his finger.

"I did some digging today, and I read the police report. No one thinks Annette killed your father. Perhaps she waited to call an ambulance, but no one can prove it. And, honestly, if that's the case, outside of turning the bastard in, Annette was the only adult in your life who had your back."

"Tell me something I don't know." The sound of a car pulling down the driveway caught her attention. She glanced over her shoulder. "Fucking wonderful. Uncle Ned is here."

"He's early," Jackson said, glancing at his watch. He took her by the hand and squeezed. "I'm not going to leave your side. I promise."

She blew out a puff of air. "I don't want him in my house."

"We'll sit outside." He tugged her toward the fire pit and arranged some of the chairs.

Her uncle slipped from the driver's side of the vehicle. God, he looked so much like her father with his chocolate eyes and salt-and-pepper hair. He'd aged some and had put on some weight, but he was still a handsome man.

He waved awkwardly as he strolled down the path. "Hi, Shannon," he said softly. "You look well."

She nodded. "This is my friend Jackson."

"I was hoping we could talk alone," Ned said.

"That won't be happening." Jackson put his arm around her. "And I know everything. So, this will be a very candid conversation."

"Wow. I'm surprised." Ned stuffed his hands into his pockets. "But relieved."

"Why relieved?" Shannon asked. "You were a part of

that life. You—"

"I was. But the day I got arrested, it changed my entire world. At first, I thought it'd ruined me, but in actuality, it set me free." He took a few steps closer.

Jackson puffed out his chest. "But you did nothing to help your niece, knowing full well—"

"I did not know my brother would bring his own daughter into that life. When I was involved, family members were off-limits."

"Oh, and that makes it okay?" Jackson said.

Shannon leaned into him, drawing on his strength.

"No. Of course, it doesn't. And anything I say will sound like an excuse. But once my brother died, I knew she was safe because there was no one to pull her in. Her mother's a lot of things, but once she was in—"

"That's bullshit," Shannon said. "Any of those men could have found me and manipulated me, and you know it." For her entire childhood, Shannon had felt as though she had no voice. Now, she felt stronger than ever.

"I was dealing with my shit, and your mother wouldn't have anything to do with me...we can go 'round and 'round with this all day, but that's not why I wanted to talk to you. You should know that Alex Angler has moved back to the area."

"You're a little too late with that juicy piece of information," Shannon said. "If that's all you wanted, why didn't you just send me an email?"

"I wanted to see you. I wanted to apologize personally. And I wanted you to know that not a day goes by that I don't regret not saying something. I needed to say that to your face. But I couldn't invade your space without your permission."

"I appreciate that." Shannon allowed the rage to fade into the background. She hadn't forgiven him for anything but holding on to it didn't help.

"How do you know about Alex?" Jackson said.

"When you went to *rehab*, as your mother spun that story, Alex and Borden came to me, wanting to know what'd happened to you."

"You'd been out of that stuff for a few years. Why did they come to you?"

"You weren't the first girl to give up a child from those sex clubs."

Jackson kicked one of the flimsy plastic chairs, sending it flying across the yard. It smacked the side of his house, shattering into pieces. "Finish what you have to say before I beat the shit out of you," he said under his breath.

"Your boyfriend is a bit of a hothead."

"Can you blame him?" Shannon asked. "He's had to watch you sit at the top of the driveway like a creeper, and now you're spouting this crap about how you wanted to tell me to my face? I'm sorry, Ned, but it wasn't necessary, and we have nothing left to say to one another." She shook out her hands. "Actually, if you had any real decency left, you would have told me the second you knew that Alex was back."

"You've said your piece, now leave." Jackson pointed. "Before I make you."

Ned held up his hands. "Alex is dangerous. He was involved in some dark shit in the city. Worse than anything your father was ever involved in."

"Oh. Because raping and selling teenagers isn't that horrible," Shannon said.

Ned cocked his head. "Be careful. He blames you for how his life turned out."

Shannon closed her eyes and waited for the sound of an engine driving away. She shivered.

"Hey, Katie," Jackson said.

Shannon blinked, glancing toward Jackson, who stood in the middle of the driveway where Ned had been parked.

"Are you following him?"

"What?" Shannon asked.

Jackson held up his finger.

"Don't shush me. Put her on speaker." The last thing Shannon needed was more secrets.

Jackson nodded.

"I'll stay with Ned until you tell me not to follow him," Katie said.

"Perfect. And what about Alex?" Jackson stared into Shannon's eyes.

"We haven't found him yet," Katie said.

"Try Alice Carson. She lives in Saratoga. According to one of my patients who recently died, her mother was screwing her boyfriend, who I suspect was Alex,"

Shannon said. "I learned that my patient had a visitor right before she killed herself, and that visitor's name was also Alex. According to the security guard who just called me, Alex was at the hospital asking questions about me. I can't imagine that those are three different men."

"I'll get my guy on it," Katie said.

"Thanks. I'm not going to leave Shannon's side until this is over." Jackson took her into his arms.

"I'd fire you as my partner if you did." The phone went dead.

"He's coming for me," Shannon whispered.

"Well, he's going to have one hell of a surprise when he does."

CHAPTER TEN

Shannon sprawled on Jackson's sofa, resting her head on his lap as she stared at the television while some movie played. She'd picked it out, but she really hadn't been paying attention. All she could think about was the man who currently ran his fingers through her hair with a tender touch.

She glanced up, catching his gaze. "Thank you."

He ran a thumb over her cheek. "For what?"

"For being so kind to me."

"That's easy to do."

She moved to a sitting position. It had been a long time since she'd had the desire to be with a man.

And not just sexually, but really invested in any kind of a relationship.

"Tell me about your ex-wife."

"Not much to tell. She's a bitch."

"You married her, so she has to have some redeeming qualities." Shannon made a bold move and sat on Jackson's lap, wrapping her arms around his shoulders, massaging gently. "One thing I know about you is that you don't jump into things without careful consideration."

He arched a brow. "That's true. And you're right about Jasmine. At first, things were good."

"So, what happened."

"She cheated on me when I was in the hospital after nearly dying."

"That sucks."

"It does. I'm not sure what was worse—the cheating or the fact that it was with my partner."

"Okay. She's a bitch, and I'm glad she's not in your life anymore."

"You and me both." He kissed her nose.

"I've really struggled most of my adult life with relationships with men. I have trust issues and—"

He pressed his finger over her lips. "I'm not surprised. What happened to you isn't easy to bounce back from. I hope you're proud of the woman you've become."

Her lips tugged into a bright smile. "I am."

"Good," he said. "As far as your issues, we all have them."

"I imagine you have some trust issues with women."

"You can say that again," he said with a hardy laugh.

"I've always prided myself on being able to read people well, and Jasmine threw me for a loop. I thought we were happy, so when I found out about the affair, I lost it. The worst part was that it started while I was in surgery. She tried to make it out to be that she thought I was dying and was looking for comfort—"

"That's a pretty lame excuse."

"I agree," she said. "How long have you been divorced?"

"My divorce only became final about six months ago. I dug my heels in and tried to take a lot of her money. Katie finally talked me into settling for a lump sum."

"And you bought *Sweet Freedom*."

"Exactly."

"That is pretty sweet."

"No. You're sweet," he whispered. "I'm struggling to remain a total gentleman when all I want to do is carry you up to my bed."

"I can walk." She stood, tugging at the hem of her shirt, lifting it over her head and tossing it across the room. It landed on the lamp.

He groaned. "Are you sure? Because I don't think I have the ability to say no when it comes to you."

She took him by the hands and helped him to his feet. "I've never been surer of anything in my life." She reached behind and unclasped her bra, letting it drop to her feet.

His eyes widened as his gaze lowered. "We might not make it upstairs."

"I'm not complaining."

He reached out and traced a path down the center of her chest. "I'm not saying this because you're standing here half-naked, but you are gorgeous." His fingers toyed with the button on the top of her jeans. He pressed his lips to the top of her breast as he lowered her zipper and removed her pants.

Normally, with any other man she'd been with, sex happened in the dark, under the sheets. The few times she'd branched out of her comfort zone, it just wasn't very good. It might have been for the men, but she was too tense to truly enjoy herself.

With Jackson, she found herself in uncharted waters.

She threaded her fingers through his thick, soft hair, guiding his mouth toward her excited nipple.

He didn't disappoint.

She arched her back, closing her eyes, letting the sensations overtake her mind, body, and soul.

His tongue glided down her stomach, circling her belly button. "Please, sit on the sofa." Gently, he guided her to the couch, removing her panties. He rested her legs over his shoulders. "I want to know what you like. Please, tell me."

"I like this."

He smiled as he lowered his head, his hands toying with her puckered nipples.

"Oh, yes." She blinked, watching him please her, something she'd never done before. She'd always been embarrassed by her sexuality. She knew in part that had to do with her past, but being with Jackson, she had to wonder if it also had to do with the kind of men she'd always chosen to be with.

Her past boyfriends had been safe.

They were the kind of men who weren't all that into anything but vanilla sex. They didn't make sexual jokes and always backed down when she said no.

One of the reasons she'd always turned Jackson down was that he'd come off like a man who enjoyed more.

And she wasn't wrong.

Only she hadn't expected that she'd be willing to push her boundaries.

Her breath caught in her chest. Her toes curled. The build came hard and fast, and she wasn't prepared for the onslaught of sensations that exploded inside her as he stroked her, bringing her to new heights.

She clutched his head, tugging at his hair. Her body convulsed. She gasped for air. Orgasms weren't a problem. She'd given herself many. And a few men had managed to find their way around her body.

But no one made her feel like this.

"Jackson," she managed with a throaty groan, her climax still gripping at her muscles. Her pulse soured out of control. "Oh, God." A second one built in the pit of her stomach. It vibrated through her veins, hitting every part of her body.

He lifted his head, kissing his way up to her mouth, which he took in a hot, wet kiss.

She tugged at the fabric of his clothing, desperate to feel his naked body against hers.

"You are amazing." He tore at his shirt, tossing it to the side. Slowly, he lowered his slacks over his hips.

Licking her lips, she adjusted herself on the sofa. Her chest heaved up and down with every deep breath. She'd never wanted anything so much in her life.

He pulled something from his pocket and held it up as he stood before her, gloriously naked. "Birth control," he said.

"Good call." She took the condom in her fingertips. "We'll use it in a second."

"What are you doing?"

"Having my own little party." Taking him into her mouth, she did something that had always been uncomfortable for her, but she'd been determined to overcome.

And she had.

But not like this.

She stroked, licked, and tasted, enjoying his harsh groans and the way his thigh muscles flexed, and his fingers brushed her hair from her forehead.

"That's enough of your party. Time to mix it up." He lifted her off her feet, spun her around, and sat on the sofa. He took the condom and tore the package open with his teeth.

Straddling him, she accepted his length as if they had always been together.

He held her by the hips, guiding her, slowly at first and then picking up speed as they gazed into each other's eyes.

"Shannon. Sweet, beautiful Shannon," Jackson whispered.

In his arms, she felt as if she'd come home. This is where she belonged, and she would do whatever it took to keep Jackson in her life.

He thrust into her hard and deep as he buried his face in her neck, kissing wildly. He groaned, holding her still as his climax spilled out.

He held her tightly, leaning back on the sofa while running his hands up and down her back. "I've fallen so hard for you, I can't see straight."

"I know what you mean."

"It's unexpected and a little scary, but I would never intentionally hurt you. Ever." He cupped her face and gazed into her eyes.

She smiled. "It's a lot scary how much I care for you. And I want you to know, you can trust me."

"That is something I'm not worried about."

She kissed his cheek. "It's time for my own personal *Sweet Freedom*."

He jerked his head back. "Are you saying you want to board my boat?"

"Yes. And I want to do it now."

"We're kind of naked."

She tilted her head. "After we get dressed. Maybe we can grab a bottle of wine. Because I might need a drink."

"Are you sure?"

"Just like being with you, I've never been so sure of anything in my life."

CHAPTER ELEVEN

S hannon stood at the edge of the dock. The moon and the stars shone over the Tartan, casting an eerie glow. She glanced over her shoulder. Jackson had raced back up to the house because he'd forgotten his cell. He waved as he stepped into his cottage.

He'd be back in less than five minutes.

The sailboat wouldn't swallow her whole in that time.

She blew out a long breath. "I can't believe I'm going to do this, but it's time I stop letting you control my world."

"That's impossible," a familiar male voice rang out.

"Who's there?" She squinted as a shadow appeared in the aft of the boat. She gasped, dropping the bottle of wine. It shattered into a million pieces around her feet. "Alex."

"In the flesh." He smiled, holding his hands out

wide. "I have to say. You've turned into quite the little sex kitten."

She swallowed her heart, then opened her mouth to say something but no words tumbled from her lips.

"Why don't you let me help you aboard this beauty?" He offered his arm. "We can start where we left off."

"That's not going to happen, and Jackson will be here any second."

"No, he won't. Your uncle Ned is taking care of him."

She clutched her pendant. "Why are you doing this?"

"Come onto the boat and—"

Bang!

She turned on her heel. "No." She took one step, but her foot landed in a pile of glass. She screamed in pain. The dock vibrated, and Alex lifted her into his arms. "Put me down, you bastard."

"Sure thing." He carried her onto *Sweet Freedom*, tossing her onto the back bench. He turned and untied the sailboat from the dock. "This is just like old times."

She jumped to her feet, only to fall to her knees. "I'll kill you before I ever let you touch me again."

"Good luck trying, you little bitch."

"What the hell did I ever do to you?" She crawled to the corner of the boat and glanced at the bottom of her foot. At least five pieces of glass stuck out. Carefully, she pulled the ones she could find.

She didn't have her cell, which meant she only had two options.

Jump.

Or kill.

Jackson glanced over his shoulder and waved before stepping into his house. He reached for his cell, which he'd left on the table by the door. Out of the corner of his eye, he saw movement.

Shit.

"We meet again," Ned said as he emerged from the kitchen.

"What the fuck are you doing in my home?" And where the hell was Katie? But he'd deal with that question in a second.

"Getting my revenge." He waved a gun in the air.

"For what?" Jackson fingered his cell, calling 9-1-1 before putting it into his back pocket and laying his hand on his weapon. Thank God he never stepped outside without it.

"A few things."

"Explain it to me. Because I'm confused about what Shannon ever did to you."

"When my brother died, I was in charge of my own club. I had people, and I was back."

"I thought you lost your wife and your job when you

were arrested and turned over a new leaf." All Jackson had to do was buy some time. Only he knew he didn't have it because he suspected that Ned wasn't alone.

"I had to act as if I did. But I also had to prove to my brother I had what it took, and he was about to let me back in. Until he up and died."

"Shannon didn't kill him."

"No, she didn't. But she's the one thing that Annette loves, and she might as well have put the final nail in my brother's coffin."

"Why not go after Annette?"

"I have different plans for Annette. But I promised Alex I'd help him first."

"Why?"

"Shannon stole everything from Alex. He was in love with her, and she wouldn't give him the time of day after Dwight died."

"That's not love." Jackson had heard enough. He didn't need to know any more about these sick, twisted, demented minds. There was no understanding their logic. But he did need to find out one thing. "I had someone following you. What happened to them?" He was very careful not to mention whether it was a male or a female, just in case Katie was hiding in the shadows somewhere.

"Spunky little redhead?"

Jackson drew his lips into a tight line.

"Seems she had a car accident."

"You're going to regret that." In one swift motion, Jackson pulled his weapon and pulled the trigger.

Bang!

He nailed Ned in the gut.

Ned dropped his handgun and doubled over.

"Stupid fucking idiot." Jackson raced across the room and snagged the Glock. He took off his shirt and handed it to Ned. "Put pressure on the wound. The cops are on the way." He pulled out his cell and spoke quickly with the operator before racing toward the waterfront.

Only his boat was about two hundred feet from shore, with the engine running.

Fuck.

"Jackson," Katie yelled from the top of the driveway.

"Thank God, you're okay."

Katie jogged down the path with a slight limp. "My car's totaled, but I'm fine. What the hell is going on here?"

"Ned is in my house, bleeding out, and Shannon is on my boat with Alex. The cops are on the way."

"We found Lilly and her mom. They were hiding out in some motel. Lilly's mom was terrified of Alex and what he'd do to her little girl. She knows she was wrong, but Lilly was reunited with her father and step-mother, and her mom wants to go back to rehab."

"That's good news."

Katie pointed to Jacob's SUV sitting in the driveway. "We can leave Jacob here. Let's take his boat and go save your girlfriend."

"Sounds good to me."

"You're not yelling at me, saying she's not your girl."

"That's because I'm officially off the market," Jackson said. "And I don't like it when assholes kidnap the chick I'm falling in love with."

———

"You're not going to get away with this," Shannon said.

"Get away with what?" Alex stood behind the steering wheel with a proud smile, just like he'd done when he was a nineteen-year-old boy and trying to impress and please her father.

"Killing my patients."

"I didn't kill them. They killed themselves. Even Belinda and her boyfriend. It was a murder-suicide. I mean, I might have helped that along a little bit, but I didn't actually pull the trigger."

"What about Gretchen?"

He shrugged. "I just gave her the drugs she wanted."

"You were fucking her mother."

"I fuck a lot of people," he said as if the world should be impressed by that.

"What about Lilly?" Shannon's heart skipped a beat. There had been no word about her yet.

"I wish I knew. I helped her mom get out of rehab, and that bitch paid me back by taking off."

Shannon let out a long breath. She prayed that was true and that Lilly was safe. "Where are we going?"

"Well, first, we're going to float and reacquaint ourselves."

"Like hell we are." She gripped the side of the bench, glancing around for something hard she could use to beat him over the head. No way would she let him touch her.

Ever.

"It always bothered me that I wasn't first when it came to you. That I had to go in second or third. Sometimes, even last. Your father would often tease—"

"I'm not listening to this bullshit. My father was a sick man, and so are you. What you did to me was criminal, and I'm not going to let you do it to me again."

"No. You're not. You're going to give yourself freely to me like you used to." He cut the engine and sat next to her, resting his hand on her thigh.

She brushed it away. "Don't ever mistake my passivity for willingness."

"You forget about the times we held each other after, and how you always smiled at me."

"I didn't hold you. You laid on top of me. Big difference." She tried to stand, but the pain in her foot forced her to the fiberglass floor.

"Oh. All fours. I can be talked into that position."

"Fucking pig." She kicked out with her good foot, landing it right between his legs.

He doubled over, groaning. "You bitch."

She hobbled toward the cabin, snagging the fire extinguisher off the side of the door.

The hum of an engine caught her attention. She glanced to the port side but saw no lights, even though she knew a boat approached.

"You're going to regret that." Alex stood and inched closer.

"The only thing I regret is not having the courage to put you and the rest of the men my father sold me to in jail." She raised the red canister and swung.

Hard.

Connected with his head.

He fell to the right, hitting the side of the boat, his body jerking backward. He laughed as he lunged forward.

She repeated the motion, this time hitting him under the chin.

He stumbled back, losing his footing and flipping over the side of the boat with a splash.

Tossing the extinguisher to the side, she raced to the back of the boat and turned the engine over. She wasn't more than a few miles from home. She gripped the wheel and came about.

A light flashed in her face.

She covered her eyes. "Jackson?" She pulled back on the throttle as a Boston Whaler appeared with Katie at the helm and Jackson standing in the bow. "Thank God. I thought you were dead."

Jackson jumped aboard *Sweet Freedom*. "Where's Alex?"

"In the water somewhere." She fell into Jackson's arms.

"I'll find him," Katie said. "And the Lake George patrol is on their way."

"There's blood everywhere," Jackson said.

"I cut my foot."

He lifted her into his arms, carried her to the bench, and sat down. "Are you okay otherwise?"

She nodded, snuggling against his body. "I am now."

"And here I thought I needed to come out here and save you, but it looks like you saved yourself."

She glanced up and stared into Jackson's loving eyes. "I did, didn't I?"

"Yeah." He kissed her tenderly. "Before I get really mushy on you, I want you to know that Lilly and her mom are safe."

"That's wonderful."

"It is," Jackson said. "I think I have to sell this boat."

"Probably a good idea. But maybe you can buy something else. I think I want to take up sailing again."

"Good. Because I need someone to teach me how."

She jerked her head back. "You bought this sucker with no idea how to sail?"

He nodded.

"That's crazy."

"What do you think is crazier? That, or the fact that I'm falling madly in love with you?"

"Oh. Definitely the sailboat." She rested her head on his chest. "Falling in love with you is going to be the best thing that has ever happened to me."

———

"You can see her now," the doctor said as he stepped into the waiting room.

"Thanks." Jackson stood, shoving his hands deep into his pockets. He hated that Shannon had to be in the same hospital as her uncle and the man who'd raped her, but at least he knew that she was safe and no one was going to hurt her again.

Not on his watch.

"What are you waiting for?" Katie asked. "Go. I'll wait for a report on her asshole uncle when he comes out of surgery."

"I don't know if I want him to die on the table, or live so he can face life in prison."

"Trust me, life in prison is the better option. Same goes for Alex," Katie said.

"Only, we don't know if they have enough on—"

"Stop," Katie said. "Right now, you should be focusing on Shannon and helping her between her torn up foot, her crazy-ass mother who is MIA, and just being the best boyfriend you can be."

Jackson's heart beat a little faster. He hadn't expected to find love and it honestly scared him, but not enough to run from it. "Thanks, Katie."

"Don't mention it. I'll call you when I know anything."

Jackson nodded as he strolled down the corridor in search of Shannon's room. He found it and pulled back the curtain.

She lifted her head and smiled. "Hey there," she said. "No sign of my mother out there, huh?"

"I'm sorry, no. I called and told her what happened, but I don't think she'll be coming." He sat on the edge of the gurney. "But if it makes you feel any better, Annette is on her way."

Shannon smiled. "That does help."

"How are you feeling?" He rested his hand on her thigh and kissed her cheek.

"You can do better than that."

"Oh. I can." He pressed his mouth against hers, slipping his tongue between her plump lips. A deep groan vibrated in his throat. "Better?"

"Much," she whispered. "What happens now?"

"As soon as we get your walking papers, I'll take you home and wait on you until you're better."

"No. I mean with Alex, my uncle, and the sex rings."

"Oh. That." Jackson ran a hand over his face. "Well, they have Alex on kidnapping charges, no problem. And your uncle with breaking and entering and assault with a deadly weapon."

"That's not enough."

Jackson nodded. "Alex is facing a plethora of charges, and Westerfield will be able to make them stick. But he does have a lot of investigating to do, and I'm going to be riding his ass every step of the way. Katie and I will be doing a lot of our own, as well. We will make sure these sex rings are closed out, and that Alex and your uncle go to jail for a very long time."

"I don't want you and Katie to spend—"

"We want to."

Shannon nodded.

"But first, I'm taking a few weeks off to pamper you and—"

"Where is she?" Annette's voice bounced in Jackson's ears.

Shannon dropped her head on his shoulder. "Do you know she lives farther away than my mom?"

"I do."

"Oh, thank God you're okay." Annette raced around to the other side of the bed and hugged them both. "I was so worried about the two of you."

"You didn't have to drive all the way up here," Shannon said.

"Of course, I did." She kissed Shannon's forehead and then Jackson's cheek. "Now, I'll leave the two of you to continue your little kissy-kissy."

Jackson laughed. "No reason for you to leave," he said. "I think Shannon and I will have plenty of time for that later."

CHAPTER TWELVE

Shannon set her foot on the pillow. So much had happened in the last twenty-four hours, she wasn't sure her head was on straight, and seeing her mother wouldn't be easy.

"There, now. That should help," Annette said. "Can I get you anything else?"

"My mom is going to freak when she sees you here."

"I can leave if you want me to."

Shannon shook her head. "If I can face down Alex, I can do this."

The sound of Jackson's feet stomping down the stairs made Shannon's heart swell.

She smiled.

"How's the patient?" he asked before bending over and giving her a kiss that should have been done in private—but who was she to complain?

"Better now," she said.

"What's the ETA on your mom?"

"About twenty," Annette said. "Are you going to stay?"

"If Shannon wants me to, of course."

"I could use all the moral support I can get. I mean, I am the morning news, and my mother didn't sound too happy that our skeletons fell out of the closet, to quote her."

"Too bad," Jackson said. "Besides, all a story like this does is help other people."

"Agreed." Annette folded her arms as she glanced out the window. "She's early."

Shannon adjusted her bangs and smoothed the front of her slacks. She told herself that, no matter what happened, she would be kind to her mother, but she'd realign her boundaries, depending on what came out of her mouth.

Annette opened the door. "Melinda, it's good to see you."

"I can't say the same," Melinda said. "Why are you here?"

"I asked her to come." Shannon waved her mother inside.

Melinda set her purse on the coffee table and glanced at Jackson. "I didn't realize we were having a little party. I was hoping to talk to you in private."

"*I* hoped you'd show more concern for my well-being." Shannon couldn't expect her mother to change her stripes in one day. And maybe she never would.

And that would have to be okay.

Melinda sat on the edge of the sofa, resting her hand on Shannon's leg. "I've been worried sick about you all night." She swiped at her cheeks. "This isn't easy for us. I wasn't even married to your father when... when...you got pregnant."

"But you knew. And you're my mother and did nothing."

Melinda gasped. "That's not true. I had no idea your father was into any of that stuff, and I have a hard time believing everything being reported now. Your dad might have cheated, but he wasn't a monster." She raised her chin. "If Alex hurt you when you were young, I'm sorry."

"If? Mother, he raped me. As did many of Daddy's friends. And if you're not going—"

"I'm not going to have this conversation with her,"—she looked at Annette—"or him,"—a glare at Jackson—"in the room," her mother said quietly.

"Then we're not going to have it at all." For the first time in Shannon's life, she felt strong enough to do what she'd always thought was impossible. "I love you, Mom. I really do. But if you can't acknowledge what happened to me, what you know deep down in your heart of hearts, then please leave."

"You had me drive all the way here just to humiliate me? It's bad enough you can't go to your fitting for your sister's wedding. Why are you so selfish?" Melinda stared at her with blank eyes.

"I think this discussion is over," Jackson said. "Your daughter said it was time to go, so I'd appreciate it if you honored her wishes."

"And who are you to my daughter?" Melinda stood with a scowl.

"The man who loves her and is willing to stand by her, no matter what. That's who." He pointed toward the door.

"If you ever want to really talk about what happened when I was a kid, Mom, I'm always willing. We could even go to therapy together. I don't want to shut you out, but if this is how it's going to be, then our relationship will be confined to family gatherings when my sisters have me over."

"This is your doing, not mine." Melinda, as graceful as ever, took her purse and left.

"You are an amazing woman. I wouldn't have been so kind." Annette closed the door.

"I'm with her on this one."

Shannon wiped the tears that she couldn't hold back. "I gave her a chance. The rest is up to her."

Jackson lifted her feet, making himself comfortable at the end of the sofa, then resting her legs on his thighs. "Annette, could you give us a few minutes?"

"Absolutely. I need to call my husband anyway." Annette stepped outside.

"What's going on? You look so serious." Shannon didn't like when Jackson rubbed his temple.

"I wanted to talk to you about your daughter."

Shannon's heart jumped to her throat. "You found her?"

"I think you should put your name in the registry and let her decide if she wants to meet you or not."

"You really did find her, didn't you?"

He nodded.

"And?"

"I only know where she is. With everything that's happened, I got sidetracked with making sure you didn't die."

Shannon clutched her pendant. "Why do you, of all people, want me to do that?"

"Because I know you. And I know you'd want it to be her call. But if you don't give her the option, she'll have a hard time finding you and might not go to the lengths I did to find her." He pulled out his cell. "I have some information about her if you want it."

She nodded. "I do. Please, tell me about her. Tell me I did the right thing."

"From what I can tell, she's had a normal childhood. She's got an older brother and a little sister—both adopted. She's a freshman in college now, studying psychology."

Shannon smiled. "Really?"

Jackson nodded as he scrolled through the report. "Wow. She looks just like you. Do you want to see?"

"I was always so afraid she'd look like one of the men, and then I'd know who he was, and that was something I couldn't deal with."

"All I see is you."

"You're biased," she said, holding out her hand. "I want to see." She took the cell, and it was like staring at herself in a mirror. "Oh, my. She even has bangs." Shannon covered her mouth. "She looks happy."

"Katie said she is."

"I don't want to intrude on her life." Shannon handed Jackson the phone. "I don't need to know her."

"What if she needs to know *you*?"

"What about your rule?"

Jackson laughed. "I think I've learned that's a stupid rule. Put your name in the registry and just remember that if she doesn't ever come looking, you loved her enough to give her better than what you had."

"You're right. I should give her that opportunity, if she wants it."

"That's my girl," Jackson said. "Now, I have a hard question for you."

"Oh. Because nothing about the last few days has been hard."

"How do you feel about having more children?"

She cocked her head. "I've never thought about it."

"I swore after Jasmine and I divorced that marriage and kids were off the table. But I'm starting to think differently. I know we've barely started being a couple, but I want to know where you stand on the subject."

Shannon pressed her hand over her stomach. She hadn't wanted to even think about doing that to her body again. During her pregnancy, she'd felt alone and lost. Even worse while she gave birth and for years after. She felt empty and lonely. Now, being with Jackson made her wonder if family might be something she *could* do. "I think it's something I'm open to in the future."

"Cool. Now, how about you make more room on this sofa, and we watch a movie? Annette brought over a dozen."

"Sounds like a plan."

He snuggled in behind her, holding her close to his chest and kissing her neck.

She belonged in his arms, and it would be forever where she remained.

No longer was she a hostage to her family's dark legacy.

" S weetheart, relax."

Shannon shook out her hands and paced. "Easy for you to say. Your daughter didn't just call you out of the blue and ask to meet you."

Jackson patted Max's back as the four-month-old fell asleep in his father's arms. "It's going to be fine."

"What if something is wrong? Like she has some horrible disease or something."

Jackson arched a brow. "You really need to stop thinking the worst when it comes to Erica."

Erica Gladstone.

That was her daughter's name, and she was twenty-two years old now—a grown adult.

Shannon glanced at her watch. They had agreed to meet in the park ten minutes ago. "Maybe she changed—"

"Shannon?" a female voice said.

"Yes." Shannon turned and came face-to-face with a young woman who looked very much like her, though she was about an inch taller, and her hair was a little darker.

"Hi. I'm…um…Erica."

"Oh. Well. Hi." Shannon fought the tears stinging her eyes. "This is my husband, Jackson. And that's our son, Max."

Erica nodded, resting her hands on a small baby bump. "My husband is sitting in the car over there. I was going to have him walk over with me, but I didn't know if that would be too much or not."

"We'd love to meet him," Jackson said as he bounced up and down. "Please. Have him come over."

"Yes. I'm sure Jackson would love a guy to talk to."

"How long have you been married?" Erica asked, glancing over her shoulder.

"Almost two years now," Shannon said.

"Why don't I take this little guy for a stroll? I can go grab your husband. What's his name?"

"John. I'm sure he'd like that. He wasn't sure if he should stay or go."

"I'll get John, and we'll go grab some coffee or something. We'll be right back."

Shannon nodded. "Shall we sit?" She waved to a park bench. "I really don't know how this works."

"Me, either." Erica laughed nervously. "Thank you for meeting me."

"I'm glad you reached out."

Erica took a seat, wiping a tear. "I have to be honest with you. When I found out I was pregnant and decided to dig into my adoption, I did a Google search when I got your name to see what I could find out on my own."

"I see." Shannon knew all too well what Erica had found. "I can only imagine what you saw on the internet. I'm sorry."

"Why are you sorry? You didn't do anything wrong." Erica reached out and took Shannon's hand. "I have to admit, when I first called the adoption agency, I didn't think I wanted anything but my records. When I read the article about what those men did to you—my birth mother—I knew I had to find you. My parents, siblings, my husband, and even his parents all agreed."

A guttural sob escaped Shannon's lips.

"I'm sorry. I didn't mean to upset you. I just wanted to tell you, in person, how much it means to me that you loved me enough to give me this life and how I wish I could have loved you back."

Tears dribbled down Shannon's cheek. "That's not what I expected to hear."

"You're a brave woman for what you did, and while I have loving parents who raised me, I'm hoping we can be friends. I want to find a way for you to be in my life. In my baby's life."

Shannon wiped her face. "I thought if you knew how you came into this world, you'd hate me."

"I hate the man who did this to you. And I don't

ever want to know my birth father, but I want to know the woman who not only had the guts to give me up—which I can't imagine was easy—but who then turned her life around and went about helping other young girls. Did I tell you I'm getting a master's in social work? I'm not exactly going into your field, but I must have gotten that passion from you. My father is a math teacher, and my mother is an accountant. I hate math."

"I failed the ninth-grade regent's exam," Shannon admitted.

"I barely passed, and my parents were always so frustrated that they had to hire a math tutor for *their* child."

Erica rubbed a hand over her stomach.

"How far along are you?"

"Almost six months. I know I'm young. And, honestly, we didn't plan this. We found out I was pregnant five days before our wedding. Total shocker." Erica smiled wide. "You should have seen the look on John's face when I told him as we were getting ready for bed and I informed him that he could toss the brand-new box of condoms he'd bought for our honeymoon into the garbage." Erica covered her mouth and giggled. "He bought like a hundred of them. I have no idea what he thought our ten-day trip to the Bahamas was going to be like, but no way in hell was he going to need that many."

"When I told Jackson he was about to be a daddy, we were on the dock and he tried to do this little jig and fell right into the lake. I almost peed my pants from laughing so hard because I'm the klutz, not Jackson." Shannon glanced at the sky, searching for the right words. "You mentioned wanting medical history."

Erica placed her hand on Shannon's leg. "I said I don't want to know my father, I meant it."

"Here's the thing, Erica. I still don't know which one of those men is your birth father, so I can't give you his medical information. But if you need me to, I will gladly find that out for you."

Erica threw her arms around Shannon and hugged her tight.

Shannon gasped. Tentatively, she squeezed her daughter back.

Her daughter.

"This is the first time I've ever held you," she whispered.

Erica cried. "They didn't let you when I was born?"

"No. And it was for the best. Really. It was." Shannon cupped Erica's face. "You are not the sum of what happened that night."

"I know that. And neither are you."

"That is true."

"Can I ask you a question?"

"Of course," Shannon said.

"What happened to all those men? I honestly focused my attention on articles about you, not them. Did they get what they deserved?"

"Thanks to my husband, they sure did." Shannon

smiled. "I don't know exactly what you read, but my uncle was involved and he's facing life in prison without prarole. One of the other men, the one who kidnapped me last year, is facing the same sentence. One of the others is dead, and the other three have all been arrested because they were still involved in some kind of sex ring." Shannon waved at Jackson as he strolled across the park, pushing their son's stroller with John at his side. The two men looked to be deep in conversation. "Jackson keeps a finger on the sex ring world and works with the police to try and put an end to as many as possible."

"I'm so sorry you had to go through that."

"But it's over now, and I have a wonderful life with Jackson." Shannon took Erica's hand. "If it's okay with you, I'd like to get to know you better. Maybe we can all have dinner sometime. However, I'll never take your mother's place or try to be one to you. I gave you up. Not because I didn't love you, because I did—I *do*—but because I couldn't be a mother at sixteen and potentially expose you to the insane world my father and uncle had dragged me into."

"I know that," Erica said. "But I see no reason why I can't have you both. Can you?"

"No, I can't." Shannon squeezed her hand. "Do you like to sail?"

"I've only been a couple of times, but John, he loves sailing."

"My husband and I have a small sailboat. You should come with us sometime."

"We'd love that."

Shannon smiled. It was time to bury all the darkness and create the kind of legacy her family could be proud of.

Thank you for taking the time to read *Dark Legacy*. Please feel free to leave an HONEST review. The next book in the series is *Legacy of Lies*. This is Katie Bateman's story.

Sign up for my Newsletter (https://dl.bookfunnel.com/ 6atcf7g1be) where I often give away free books before publication.

Join my private Facebook group (https://www.facebook.com/ groups/191706547909047/) where I post exclusive excerpts and discuss all things murder and love!

And on Bookbub: bookbub.com/authors/jen-talty

ABOUT THE AUTHOR

Jen Talty is the *USA Today* Bestselling Author of Contemporary Romance, Romantic Suspense, and Paranormal Romance. In the fall of 2020, her short story was selected and featured in a 1001 Dark Nights Anthology. She is currently contracted to write in the *With Me in Seattle* series by Kristen Proby with Lady Boss Press, as well as Susan Stoker's *Special Forces: Operation Alpha* and Elle James's *Brotherhood Protectors.*

Regardless of the genre, her goal is to take you on a ride that will leave you floating under the sun with warmth in your heart. She writes stories about broken heroes and heroines who aren't necessarily looking for romance, but in the end, they find the kind of love books are written about :).

She first started writing while carting her kids to one hockey rink after the other, averaging 170 games per year between 3 kids in 2 countries and 5 states. Her first book, IN TWO WEEKS was originally published in 2007. In 2010 she helped form a publishing company (Cool Gus Publishing) with *NY Times* Bestselling Author Bob Mayer where she ran the technical side of the business through 2016.

Jen is currently enjoying the next phase of her life...the empty nester! She and her husband reside in Jupiter, Florida.

Grab a glass of vino, kick back, relax, and let the romance roll in...

Sign up for my Newsletter (https://dl.bookfunnel.com/6atcf7g1be) where I often give away free books before publication.

Join my private Facebook group (https://www.facebook.com/groups/191706547909047/) where I post exclusive excerpts and discuss all things murder and love!

And on Bookbub: bookbub.com/authors/jen-talty

PLAYING WITH FIRE

PRIVATE CONVERSATION

THE RIGHT GROOM

AFTER THE FIRE

CAUGHT IN THE FLAMES

The Men of Thief Lake

REKINDLED

DESTINY'S DREAM

Federal Investigators

JANE DOE'S RETURN

THE BUTTERFLY MURDERS

The Aegis Network

THE LIGHTHOUSE

HER LAST HOPE

THE LAST FLIGHT

THE RETURN HOME

THE MATRIARCH

The Collective Order

THE LOST SISTER

THE LOST SOLDIER

THE LOST SOUL

THE LOST CONNECTION

Hot Hunks

Cove's Blind Date Blows Up

My Everyday Hero – Ledger

Tempting Tavor

Holiday Romances

A CHRISTMAS GETAWAY

<u>ALASKAN CHRISTMAS</u>

WHISPERS

CHRISTMAS IN THE SAND

CHRISTMAS IN JULY

Heroes & Heroines on the Field

TAKING A RISK

TEE TIME

The Twilight Crossing Series

THE BLIND DATE

SPRING FLING

SUMMER'S GONE

WINTER WEDDING

Witches and Werewolves

LADY SASS

ALL THAT SASS

Coming soon! NEON SASS

Coming soon! PAINTING SASS